"I'm askin[g] ... Laura.

"I realize I may not be the best of marriage prospects. Yet surely you realize I'd do my best to give you the life you deserve."

Laura tried not to lose sight of what was important. He hadn't mentioned love, she thought fiercely. She felt that if she and Enzo reached for happiness, disaster would result.

"Aren't you going to answer?" he asked. "I love you so much."

The words twisted in her heart. Could she believe them? Was Enzo the trustworthy man she wanted him to be? Or merely a pragmatist given to pretty speeches?

Suzanne Carey is a former reporter and magazine editor who prefers to write romance novels because they add to the sum total of love in the world.

MARRY ME AGAIN

BY
SUZANNE CAREY

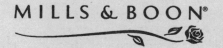

MILLS & BOON®

*MILLS & BOON and MILLS & BOON with the Rose Device
are registered trademarks of the publisher.*

*First published in Great Britain 1998
Harlequin Mills & Boon Limited,
Eton House, 18-24 Paradise Road, Richmond, Surrey, TW9 1SR*

© Verna Carey 1994

ISBN 0 263 80829 7

*Set in Times Roman 10 on 11.5pt.
02-9806-57190 C1*

*Printed and bound in Great Britain
by Mackays of Chatham PLC, Chatham*

Chapter One

Would it happen again? Or had the experience that had so disturbed and shaken her the previous afternoon been a figment of her imagination? Surely the unaccustomed dizziness, the buzzing in her ears, the panorama of lights and colors that had interrupted and distorted her vision, had flowed not from the uncanny pull exerted by a small, gold-framed portrait of a brooding sixteenth-century Italian nobleman, but from the antihistamine she'd taken to tame a summer cold, along with a carelessly skipped breakfast.

Thirty-three-year-old widow Laura Rossi had returned to a bench in Regenstein Hall at the Art Institute of Chicago with the express purpose of finding out. Yet as she stared once more into the nobleman's moody dark eyes, her sketchpad lying forgotten in her lap, she was aware that her unsettled feelings owed less to curiosity than to obsession.

The painting was part of a celebrated international traveling show of Renaissance works. She'd initially viewed it a week earlier, when she'd come to the museum in search of ideas for Rossi Originals' winter collection. Since then, she'd revisited the show three times, in order to make additional sketches. At least that was what she'd told Carol Merchant, her friend and business partner in the fledgling fashion-design firm she'd founded after her husband's death.

In truth, she hadn't been able to stay away. She couldn't seem to get enough of looking at the portrait's subject, an intense-looking man about forty years of age who wore a black velvet doublet with a narrow white ruffle at the throat and held a pair of supple leather gloves in graceful but powerful-looking fingers. The man himself was anonymous. According to the printed card that accompanied it, his likeness had been executed by a little-known Piedmontese master around 1520, some 440 years before her birth. Yet it was as if she knew him well—*had* known him for as long as she could remember.

Genuine recognition wasn't possible, of course, given the span of centuries that separated them. The only link she could hypothesize was the fact that her late husband, race car driver Guy Rossi, had hailed from the same general area in northern Italy where the portrait had been painted. It was a tenuous one, at best. Guy, whose complete baptismal name had been Guillermo Pietro Antonio da Sforza Rossi, had been estranged from his wealthy industrialist father by the time they'd met. She'd never set foot in the land of his birth, never visited the family-owned auto works in Turin, or the Rossi villa in the nearby countryside.

To further discredit her theory, there was scant physical resemblance or seeming similarity of temperament between the man she'd married and the minor Renaissance nobleman whose portrait fascinated her so much. Whereas Guy had been slim, fair and easygoing, the man in the portrait was dark, with a compact, muscular physique. His expression hinted at black moods and periodic flashes of temper. She sensed a capacity for deep-seated emotion.

The spell of vertigo she'd suffered, and the haunting sense of familiarity she felt, weren't the only phenomena connected with his painted image that troubled her. When the portrait had appeared to disintegrate before her eyes the day before, something else had happened, too. She'd had what she could only call intimations of another time and place—seeing and hearing barely discerned shapes and colors, sound, light and movement. Incredibly, she'd glimpsed high-ceilinged rooms and damask curtains. Her skin had prickled at the lush sensation of velvet fabric brushing against her arm.

Though she was the creative type, an art major who made her living marketing the products of an inborn gift for line and color and a sprightly ingenuity, she hadn't previously had what she would term a psychic or paranormal experience. She was far from certain she wanted to have another. Yet the adventurer in her was determined to discover whether the bizarre sensations and elusive images that had alarmed and dazzled her would be repeated.

Guided by one of the museum's volunteer docents, a tour group composed of a half-dozen middle-aged couples was making its way along one side of the gallery. As Laura continued to contemplate the portrait, their bodies momentarily blocked her view. For her, it was as if a tether had snapped, or a laser beam had been cut in half. When the group moved on, a minute or two later, "contact" was reestablished. An illusion fashioned of pigment and varnish on canvas, the nobleman's gaze seemed to pierce hers like a lance.

It was almost closing time. The tour group exited the gallery and, little by little, the museum's other patrons began drifting toward the exits. Before long, Laura was alone in the room. I ought to be going, too, she thought reluctantly. It's just a portrait, after all. An inanimate object, incapable of causing time to waver. Besides, Paolo will be hungry. And Josie will be waiting to go home to her teenage brood.

Abruptly, as if in mocking response to her eagerness to dismiss what had happened on her previous visit, her ears began to buzz. Seconds later, she gripped the edges of her bench as the portrait's solid reality trembled. Instead of a gallery where she was the sole remaining occupant, she beheld—dimly, as if through the diaphanous filter of a semi-sheer curtain—a classically proportioned salon with painted frescoes. Moving figures in the costumes of another time crowded her peripheral vision. Tantalizing murmurs in what she took to be an archaic Italian dialect wove themselves like ribbons through the gauzy air.

Seconds later, it might never have been. The portrait coalesced, striking her perception once more as a solid object. No longer haunted by apparitions hovering just beyond her reach, the gallery was empty of specters and reverberations.

Unnerved, she struggled to get a grip on herself. Your imagination is playing tricks on you again, she asserted shakily. You *willed* that scene to unfold. Something in your head created it. In the face of all that was rational, her sensing, feeling nature argued otherwise. To it, the apparition or vision that had overwhelmed her was devastatingly real, as prone to reinvade her consciousness as an influenza virus to cause a relapse. She'd have screamed if someone had come up behind her and touched her or spoken at that moment. Taking a deep breath, she got to her feet, picked up her sketchpad and slung the strap of her soft cognac leather purse over her shoulder. A few minutes later, she was walking past the museum's front desk in her blue-and-white cotton blouse and flowing denim skirt and going outside to wait for her bus beneath one of the lion statues that flanked its entrance. Still incredulous, she gazed at the throng of pedestrians who shared the sunlit steps with her, the traffic on Michigan Avenue, without really seeing them.

Her bus came and, as if in a trance, she boarded it. Sunk in reflection as they edged northward, their progress impeded by rush-hour traffic, she stared at the Chicago River bridge, Tribune Tower and the glittering boutiques of the city's most exclusive shopping district as if they formed a painted, illusory backdrop to her private thoughts.

Somehow she remembered to get off at the correct stop. Her third-floor apartment in a converted DePaul-area brownstone was situated several blocks to the west.

Green-eyed like her, with the remnants of baby fat still softening his little-boy contours, her four-year-old son Paolo ran to Laura when she unlocked the door.

"Mommy! Mommy!" he cried as, shrugging off speculation, she bent to hug him. "Come and see! Josie and I finished building my new racetrack!"

Josie Mitchell, the divorced, middle-aged DePaul graduate student Laura had hired to baby-sit Paolo half days, between his Montessori classes and her customary return from work around 6:00 p.m., gave him an affectionate look. "I'm afraid it takes up most of the living room, Laura," she admitted with a grin. "Oh, before I forget . . . there was a man at the door about an hour ago, asking for you."

Maybe she was being hypersensitive as a result of her experience a short time earlier. But Laura didn't think so. She knew Josie well enough to detect a hint of something out of the ordinary in her tone. "Did he leave his name? Or say what he wanted?" she asked, a bit more keenly than the situation might otherwise have warranted.

Josie shook her head. "He said he'd catch you later. But maybe I can offer a clue. Though he spoke perfect English, he had some kind of foreign accent."

Her intuition thoroughly aroused, Laura posed a silent question.

"Italian, I think," the baby-sitter supplied, telling her exactly what she'd expected to hear.

Not Renaissance-era Italian, I hope! Laura thought. Of course, it was crazy to think there could be a connection.

"He was awfully good-looking," Josie added. "The kind of man you'd notice in a crowd. And wonder what was going through his head."

Making out Josie's paycheck was a weekly Friday-night event. Handing it to her, and wishing the baby-sitter a good weekend, Laura took the time to praise the racetrack Paolo had constructed for his miniature sports cars and watch a demonstration of its use before disappearing into the kitchen to start supper.

Wondering who her anonymous caller had been, and glancing occasionally at her closed sketchpad, which she'd placed on the end of the breakfast bar, she opened a jar of the prepared spaghetti Paolo liked best and began heating its contents in the microwave. With the pasta, she decided, he'd have green beans, cottage cheese and his favorite, applesauce. It's possible the nobleman was one of Guy's and Paolo's distant ancestors, she thought as she got out the makings of a chef's salad for herself and poured her son an icy-cold glass of milk. Maybe that's the resonance I felt.

If there *was* a relationship, she probably wouldn't be able to verify it. Guy's relatives weren't likely to be much help. Except for an occasional letter to his mother, Guy had broken off all contact with his family after he and his father had quarreled. There had been no answer when she'd written Anna Rossi after the accident to inform the family of his death.

According to what Guy had told her, the breach with his father had resulted from his choice of a career. In essence, Umberto Rossi, CEO and major stockholder of Rossi Motorworks, had bitterly denounced racing as a sport for playboys and insisted that Guy settle down to work in the family business. When Guy had refused, Umberto had disinherited him. If the old man hadn't permitted his wife to respond with simple condolences, he'd hardly be disposed to answer Laura's questions.

Seating Paolo on a stool at the breakfast bar with one of his toy race cars placed beside his plate as an incentive to finish his meal, Laura poured herself a glass of wine and began throwing her salad together. The best thing you could do would be to put what happened today out of your mind, she admonished herself. And stay away from the gallery until the Renaissance show is history. You have more than enough sketches to get started on the collection.

Try as she would, she couldn't dismiss the notion she had of diverse forces connected with the portrait coalescing and gathering strength. It was almost as if, behind the scenes, the fragments of light and color into which it had dissolved were continuing to shudder and dance, inexorably forming a mosaic whose completed pattern her soul would recognize.

She glanced up sharply when someone rang the doorbell. Was it her unknown visitor? Or just the paperboy, taking up his end-of-the-month collection? The latter, she guessed.

"Eat... Don't make spaghetti racecourses with your food, darling," she exhorted her blond-haired child as she snatched up her purse.

A moment later, she was sliding back the safety panel that allowed her to view whoever was standing on her doorstep. And gasping at the sight that met her eyes. It can't be, she thought. I must be losing it. Yet there he was. Incredibly, her caller, a medium-tall, dark-haired man in an expensive raw silk business suit, was the modern, flesh-and-blood equivalent of her Renaissance nobleman.

The safety window was constructed of one-way glass, and he couldn't see her. But he'd heard the panel slide back. Without question, he knew he was being observed.

"Laura Rossi?" he asked.

Parted in shock, her lips couldn't seem to form an answer. Her everyday life with her son, and the mind-bending experience she'd had that afternoon, seemed to merge, causing the solid ceramic tiles of her foyer to offer the questionable purchase of a peat bog beneath her feet.

"I'm your husband's brother, Enzo," the caller added. "From Italy. May I come in? I've come a very long way to speak with you."

Never quick to admit a stranger to her apartment under any circumstances, Laura felt rooted to the spot. How can he be Guy's brother, she wondered? Everything about him radiates a sixteenth-century ambience.

To prove his identity and good intentions, he held up his passport, which he opened to his photograph, followed by a snapshot of himself with Guy that had been taken a decade earlier. In the snapshot, they stood in shirtsleeves and rumpled slacks, smiling for the camera with their arms about each other's shoulders and their backs to a sleek, low-slung automobile beneath overarching trees.

As it happened, a copy of the identical snapshot had been among the few possessions Laura's late husband had taken with him when he stormed out of the family home near Turin some eight years earlier. It seemed the well-dressed stranger who'd come calling was exactly who he professed to be—Guy's older brother, scion of the Rossi family and heir apparent of its elite sports and racing car firm.

Gooseflesh skidding down her arms, she opened the door and stepped back, allowing him to enter. Soberly his dark eyes bridged the four-inch disparity in their heights. "You *are* Guy's widow, Laura, I presume?"

She nodded.

His voice was cultivated and deep, and his English was as flawless as Josie had described it. The cadences of his native Italy only added music. More firmly sculptured than handsome in a conventional sense, his looks were everything Paolo's baby-sitter had claimed.

Searching his face in turn, Laura breathed a tentative sigh of relief. On closer inspection, the man who'd introduced himself as Guy's brother wasn't the Renaissance nobleman's double after all. Only his eyes, and the singular intensity they contained, could be said to mirror those of the man in the velvet doublet. Why, then, did her feeling that they were kindred spirits—if not one and the same person, as she'd first thought—stubbornly persist?

Belatedly she extended her hand. "Please forgive me, Signor Rossi. It's just that... you looked so familiar. And we've never met."

She was much prettier than the young expectant mother in the photograph Guy had shown him when he and his brother met briefly at a Florida racetrack a few months before Guy's death. Enzo noted big green eyes, naturally curly shoulder-length brown hair, the kind of mouth that made a man want to kiss it. He, too, felt as if he should know her. Or rather that he did, but couldn't remember where or when they'd been introduced.

His mouth curved. "What could be more natural, given my family resemblance to my brother?"

Though she was able to detect only a faint similarity, at best, Laura was too polite to contradict him. She realized to her dismay that offering to shake hands with him had been a mistake. Whether real or imagined, the inexplicable affinity with the Renaissance nobleman she'd glimpsed in his eyes reverberated almost as compellingly in his touch. What's the matter with you? she asked silently. He's Guy's brother. Try not to make a fool of yourself.

She sighed as Enzo released her hand, his attention captured by a collection of oversize photos that decorated the wall above her living room couch. The photos, which Laura had had enlarged and framed after her husband's accident, depicted highlights of his racing career. In them, Guy looked carefree, dazzling—and, in retrospect, heartrendingly vulnerable to his fate.

A muscle worked along Enzo's jaw as he gazed at them. Little brother, he thought with a painful inward shake of his head. You'll never know how much I miss you. Why, oh, why, did you have to die and leave us that way? For him, the rift that had driven Guy to emigrate to the U.S. four years prior to his accident had made his loss even more difficult to bear.

Aware of the emotion he couldn't suppress, Laura felt her resentment over the way her late husband's family had treated him come to the fore. If Enzo cared for Guy so much, why didn't he visit him in America, she wondered? Or do what he could to patch up the rift between him and their father? If the power he exudes isn't just for show, effecting a reconciliation wouldn't have been beyond his reach.

Just then, Paolo called out to her from the kitchen. "Mommy," he piped in his little-boy voice, "what's taking you so long? Who are you talking to?"

As if it had been a mirage, Enzo's bleak expression fled. "Your son," he said, his voice filled with genuine warmth and anticipation.

"Yes." Her answer was subdued. "His name's Paolo."

"Guy wrote our mother of his impending birth shortly before the crash that claimed his life. I'd like very much to meet him."

His presence filled up her apartment in a way that made her edgy, to say the least. Yet she couldn't get enough of looking at him. She supposed it was little enough to ask. "Please . . . come this way," she replied, motioning to him to follow her.

Paolo's eyes widened as they walked into the kitchen, making it clear to anyone with half a brain that his mother didn't usually entertain male visitors. "Who are you?" the child asked, staring up at the dark-haired stranger.

To Enzo, despite the green eyes he'd inherited from his mother, Paolo was the living image of the towheaded younger brother who'd followed him everywhere when they were six and three years of age, respectively. A smudge of tomato sauce at the corner of Paolo's mouth only strengthened the notion. Though he'd never felt that way about his sister Cristina's son, his longing to sweep Paolo up in his arms was fierce and deep.

"This is your uncle Enzo, your daddy's brother," Laura explained when the man at her side didn't speak.

Except through the medium of photography, Paolo had never known his father. And Laura didn't have a brother. Unfamiliar with the basic concept of where an uncle fitted into the scheme of things, Paolo continued to stare.

Gravely Enzo grasped his boy's softly rounded fingers and shook hands with him as if he were an adult. "I'm very happy to meet you, *nipote mio*," he said. "You're a fine-looking boy. If you're anything like your father, you'll grow up to be a loving, courageous man someday."

Glancing at Laura, he caught her sudden sheen of tears. "I've interrupted your dinner hour," he observed quietly, tucking away her spontaneous twinge of grief for future reference. "Perhaps I should leave, and come back later...."

Though he'd compounded her disorientation of that afternoon, she didn't want him to go. Aside from Paolo and her parents, who were always off on an archaeological dig somewhere, she had few relatives. His praise of Guy and his warmth toward Paolo had crept past her defenses.

"That won't be necessary," she said, tentatively reaching into the cupboard for a second wineglass. "If you haven't eaten yet, perhaps you'd care to join us."

Enzo's face lit in a flash of a smile that relieved its severity. "You're sure? I'd be delighted. I hope you won't mind—" he glanced in wry amusement at Paolo's plate "—if I pass on the 'spaghetti' in favor of sharing your salad. Such pasta for a *paisan* to eat!"

A tad more comfortable in his presence than she'd been at first, Laura didn't take offense. "He prefers it." She shrugged. "I used to cook from scratch for your brother. But I don't bother much, these days."

They settled at the counter with their salads and the wine, a valpolicella Enzo praised for its dry fruitiness. As they ate romaine and Boston lettuce enlivened by cherry tomatoes, carrots, salad peppers and strips of salami and cheese, Laura filled him in on the basic details of her life with Guy, some of which he already knew, and told him of Paolo's birth and upbringing and her career without touching on her own loneliness. Perhaps he sensed it. Though her conviction that he was intense and capable of anger didn't diminish, she awarded him points for responding gently, validating with little nods and undivided attention everything she told him.

A man of obvious wealth and polish, who was probably used to fine china, sterling-silver tableware and antique crystal, he looked somewhat out of place in her attractive but modest kitchen. Yet he seemed completely at ease, as if eating at a Formica-topped counter were a habit with him.

During the occasional lull in their conversation, he watched Paolo and casually inspected his surroundings, as if noting them for future reference. At one point his hand rested on the cover of Laura's sketchbook. He seemed about to open it and flip through the pages when she poured out coffee and offered him a cup, distracting him. A moment later, she'd placed it out of reach, atop the refrigerator, because she didn't want to get into a discussion with him about the sixteenth-century nobleman it contained.

At her suggestion, they took their coffee into the living room. Paolo returned to his precious racetrack, *vroom*ing and screeching in imitation of sorely tested brakes as his miniature vehicles negotiated a series of hairpin turns.

"The race cars were a gift from Guy," Laura explained as she pulled a photo album from the bookcase.

"But I thought..."

"He started collecting them 'for his son' as soon as he found out I was expecting."

Their knees close but not touching, they sat on the couch beneath her photo wall and began leafing through the album, which was arranged in chronological order. The first several pages contained snapshots mutual friends had taken of her and Guy when they were dating. They were followed by wedding shots, racecourse photos, and a series of flattering, tenderly composed amateur portraits Guy had taken of Laura when she was pregnant.

"It's easy to see from these photos how much my brother loved you," Enzo remarked, raising moody dark eyes to hers. "The pictures speak so eloquently of it."

Caught off guard, Laura was buffeted by a sudden, powerful ground swell of emotion. Unwilling to share it with him, she quickly changed the subject. "I can't help wondering," she said, "if you came all the way from Italy on our account."

Enzo took a sip of his coffee, which was aromatic and freshly ground. "Not entirely, I'm afraid," he admitted. "I'm scheduled to fly to Detroit the day after tomorrow, to negotiate with one of your American automakers, with whom Rossi Motorworks is considering a limited joint venture. But I was hoping..."

His words trailed off uncertainly as he regarded her.

Despite the barricades she'd long since erected against caring whether the Rossis had any interest in her son, Laura couldn't hide her hurt pride and irritation. After the way Guy's family treated him, she thought, I should have known meeting Paolo wasn't his primary objective.

"The fact is, I've wanted to seek you out for some time, and my mother passed on your address," he added, as if he'd guessed what was on her mind.

Her wariness didn't abate. "What made you decide to do so now? Guy's been dead four years. You must make periodic business trips to America."

"You're right. I do."

"Then?"

Stubborn and passionate-looking, his mouth made a little moue of regret. "My father's ill, but I don't want you to think it's the only reason."

Spare me, Laura thought with displeasure. After the way Umberto behaved, you can't expect us just to forgive and forget.

"Is the problem related to his blood pressure?" she asked, attempting to focus their conversation on detail as a way of keeping the subject at arm's length. "Guy told me it was elevated. Part of the reason he didn't go back to Italy or attempt to contact his father after their falling-out was that he didn't want to upset him ... cause him to burst a blood vessel...."

The moment the words were out, she regretted them. To her ears, it sounded as if she were apologizing for her husband.

Enzo didn't seem to take them in that light. "I'm afraid so," he answered. "He's had a series of strokes ... none terribly severe alone. But their net effect has been devastating. His speech and mobility have been sadly impaired. For the past several months, he's been confined to bed. It's my belief he's dying. You know, Laura..."

Unwilling to have him continue, she all but held her breath.

So like those in the portrait, Enzo's dark eyes plumbed hers, as if to lay bare her thoughts. She had the distinct impression that he wanted to catch her by the shoulders to make his point.

"In Italy," he went on at last, obviously choosing his words with care, "family is of the utmost importance. Yes, I know what you're thinking. If that's true, why didn't my father extend an olive branch to the son he loved so much? I can only tell you that he's very proud. And, despite the wisdom of a lifetime, sometimes foolish. I realize that's no excuse. But I ask you, are we doomed to repeat his mistakes? Must the tear in our family's fabric be perpetuated?"

Still angry on Guy's behalf, she didn't want to agree with him. Yet Enzo had included her when he spoke of his family. Made it sound as if she and Paolo were part of it.

"I'm not sure what you're driving at," she whispered.

"Ah, but I think you are. I wouldn't blame you if you told me my father can go to hell. Yet I'm hoping you won't do that. Surely you must realize anger won't bring Guy back. Or heal his differences with Umberto, in a temporal sense. I can't help thinking it would be a redemption of sorts if Paolo could meet his grandfather... before it's too late."

Cornered by his reasonableness, Laura didn't know how to answer him.

"It's a great deal for me to ask, particularly on such short acquaintance," Enzo added. "But is it possible you and your son would consider paying him a visit? Naturally, the trip would be at my expense."

Her mind reeling, Laura threw up a protective barricade. "Has Umberto asked to see my son?" she demanded, going straight for what she sensed was the weakest point in his argument.

"Not exactly," he acknowledged. "I didn't mention my plan to look you up—in part to avoid raising false hopes. But, as my father's closest confidant, and the man who runs

Rossi Motorworks on his behalf, I'm convinced I can read his heart.''

Not good enough, Laura retorted silently. Though he's dead and gone, Guy deserves an apology. If I have anything to say about it, he's going to get it.

"The way things stand," she said, "I can't believe we'd get a very warm reception."

To her surprise, Enzo dropped the subject. They didn't return to it as they finished going through the album. By the time they'd closed its cover, Paolo's *vroom*ing and screeching over his toy cars had died back to a moderate level. Though he continued to put his favorite yellow Maserati through its paces, he was yawning and rubbing at his eyes.

"Time for bed, darling," Laura announced, putting the album aside and getting to her feet.

At her words, Enzo stood, also. He ruffled Paolo's hair. "I'd better be going," he said.

Allowing Paolo to play with his race cars a moment longer, Laura saw Enzo to the door.

"I can't tell you what this evening has meant," he said, turning when they reached it, so that he was standing in close proximity to her. "Meeting you and Paolo at last...it's been wonderful."

In response, a wave of familiarity washed over her. It's his eyes, she reaffirmed. They're so dark, so expressive of the bond I can't explain but strongly sense.

"I'm glad you came," she answered. "I know Guy would approve."

A little silence rested between them, poignant with their shared memory of Laura's late husband. Yet by now her grief had mostly been laid to rest. Though she'd done very little dating as a single mother, she was far from immune to Enzo's passionate but restrained appeal.

"Tomorrow's Saturday," he said, cutting across her thoughts. "Do you have to work? If not, perhaps we could spend some additional time together. I'd like to take you and Paolo out to breakfast and perhaps for an excursion to the local zoo?''

Laura didn't want to say goodbye, either. Linked in her mind with the Renaissance nobleman's portrait and her extraordinary reaction to it, Enzo's appearance on her doorstep had raised some riveting, and as yet unanswered, questions.

"I'm sure Paolo would enjoy that," she murmured, attributing her acceptance to a wish to please her little boy. "He's positively crazy about lions, tigers and elephants."

Enzo smiled, the laugh lines beside his mouth softening its intensity. "I'll pick you up around 9:00 a.m., then, if that's all right."

"We'll be waiting."

He offered his hand. A bit apprehensively, she took it. To her embarrassment, the perfunctory contact was even more electric than it had been on his arrival—as deep and soul-shattering as a kiss.

For a heartbeat, neither of them moved or spoke. Though it was the height of insanity, she could feel the barely glimpsed figures that had peopled Regenstein Hall that afternoon hovering nearby.

Just when she thought she couldn't bear the emotional pressure of their silent interchange a moment longer, Enzo broke the spell. "Good night, Laura," he told her in his deep, rich baritone, letting her fingers slip from his grasp as if with great reluctance. "I trust you and my charming nephew will sleep well."

Chapter Two

In her dream, Laura stood on the second-floor balcony of what she sensed was a stately residence. The hem of her high-waisted velvet gown descended to her ankles. Permitted to curl loosely about her shoulders in her waking life, her hair was pulled back from her forehead and constrained beneath a sheer organdy cap. Only a narrow fringe of carefully crimped ringlets escaped it to frame the pale oval of her face.

It was dusk, that transitory state between light and dark, seeing and not-seeing, so evocative of melancholy and secrets. Somewhere a dove called to its mate. Already the formally landscaped garden at her feet, which radiated from a fountain at its center to blend with a rolling, partially wooded terrain, was awash in shadows and looming shapes.

In the drawing room at her back, servants had lit the candles. Their subdued radiance spilled out to the balcony, creating a chiaroscuro effect. Someone began to play the mandolin, selecting a tune in a minor key. She caught the rustling of women's skirts, husky male whispers.

By now the day's heat had fled. Shivering a little with the encroaching chill, she became aware that she was waiting for someone. With the thought, she heard the tattoo of approaching hoofbeats. Seconds later, a rider came into view. Though she couldn't see him well, her pulse fluttered with anticipation as a servant stepped forward to help him dismount.

With a brusque command to the groom concerning his mount, he entered below, and she turned toward the house expectantly. Beyond the open floor-to-ceiling French windows that gave onto the balcony, a gala was in full sway. Men and women were laughing, talking and dancing as the mandolin player bent over his instrument.

The new arrival appeared and made his way toward her through the crowd. With the revelers' colorful finery as a foil, his black traveling cloak was somber as a crow's wing. Yet she caught a troubling flash of scarlet beneath it. Moody and willfully cast, his features were those of her sixteenth-century aristocrat.

A name sprang to her lips, one she knew but couldn't articulate. Joining her on the balcony, he caught her by the wrist. She trembled suddenly as his fingers bit into her flesh, aware that this was a case of mistaken identity.

In response, scorn curled his lip. "Not him," he said. "*Me*. Are you disappointed?"

She awoke to find herself safe at home in her apartment, in bed. Her heart was chugging like a piston of a locomotive. One of her pillows was on the floor. The sheets were tangled as if she'd just engaged in a boxing match.

Innocuous and cheerful, sunlight poured in through the windows. Sitting up and hugging her knees through her lightweight comforter, she tried to make sense of the scenario her unconscious mind had created. She'd thought the man in the dream her Italian nobleman. And then realized he wasn't. Fear had been the result. Was it possible there were *two* men who looked that way? What in God's name was happening?

Seconds later, the dream events were evaporating from her thoughts. "Oh my gosh!" she exclaimed, abruptly snatching up the digital clock she'd turned facedown on the nightstand to obscure its blue glow and scanning its face.

It was 8:32 a.m. And she'd forgotten to set her alarm. Guy's appealing, paradoxical brother would be on their doorstep in less than half an hour. She'd have to pour on the steam if she hoped to be ready by then.

An early riser, Paolo was sitting quietly on the living room rug, eating whole-grain cereal directly from the box and watching cartoons on television. "Come quick, darling!" she urged, wondering frantically what to wear and hoping against hope her brother-in-law was running late. "We have to get dressed. Uncle Enzo is taking us out to breakfast and to the zoo."

Thanks to relentless prodding on her part, they were ready with several minutes to spare. Checking her appearance in the mirror over her vanity, Laura affirmed that the powder-pink silk slacks and matching V-neck cotton sweater she'd chosen pointed up the reddish highlights in her shoulder-length brown hair. For his part, Paolo looked spiffy in jeans and a navy-and-white pullover.

Appearing promptly on the hour, Enzo smiled a hello when she slid back the safety panel and then threw open the door for him. Clad in gray linen trousers and a light yellow polo shirt that set off his dark good looks, he appeared younger, more relaxed, than she remembered. He's got to be about thirty-eight, she realized as she greeted him. Guy would have been thirty-five, and he's three years older. He doesn't look it this morning, though.

The sensual pull he exerted on her hadn't diminished. In fact, as she and Paolo accompanied him downstairs, to where his rental car was cavalierly double-parked by the curb, she had to admit it had strengthened. Just the light pressure of his hand beneath her elbow as he helped them into the off-white Mustang convertible was enough to cause her nerve endings to tingle.

What *is* it with my fascination with Rossi men? she asked herself ruefully as they shot into traffic, headed for—according to Enzo—the Hotel Nikko and its sumptuous weekend breakfast buffet. Whatever the reason, she'd do well to get it under control. Since she didn't plan to travel with her son to Italy, she doubted that, after today, she'd see her enigmatic brother-in-law again.

Fortunately for Paolo, who loathed fish and liked his eggs scrambled, the sleek Japanese hotel featured American, as well as international, dishes on its elegantly appointed hot table. Though she passed the place periodically, Laura hadn't eaten there before. During the first several years of its existence, Rossi Originals had been a shoestring operation, and she hadn't been able to afford it. Now that she could, she didn't have a ready escort.

Watching Enzo as he wielded his fork in the European manner, peeled an orange for dessert and drank *café filtre* at the end of his meal, she supposed he was what could safely be called a man of the world. It went without saying that he possessed the means to qualify. According to Guy, his family was loaded. The wafer-thin gold Patek Philippe watch Enzo wore confirmed it. So, she guessed, did his salary as de facto head of Rossi Motorworks.

A wisp of her dream invaded her thoughts, and she wondered if Enzo had been the cloaked traveler who'd baited her. Instinct argued that he hadn't. Yet she sensed with the deepest kind of knowing that his arrival in Chicago and her experience with the portrait at the Art Institute were some-how related.

After breakfast, they headed up the outer drive, past Oak Street Beach, getting off at the Fullerton Avenue exit. Incredibly, they found a parking space. As they got out of the car, Enzo unobtrusively removed a cardboard box tied with string from its trunk.

"What's that?" Paolo asked at once.

"You'll see," Enzo replied mysteriously. He glanced at Laura, his mouth curving with anticipation. "There *are* ponds at this zoo, I trust?"

Though the admission was free, he made a generous donation on their behalf at the gate. As they walked the zoo's curving paths, pausing to *ooh* and *aah* over lions and polar bears and elephants, Laura speculated that, to the casual observer, they must look like a tightly knit family group. Her hunch was confirmed a short time later when, after buying them paper cups of hot chocolate from a vendor, Enzo led them to a bench beside a duck pond and allowed Paolo to unwrap his present—a wonderful blue-and-gold toy sailboat.

"Your little boy reminds me of my grandson, who lives in California," an elderly woman remarked to Enzo from the adjoining bench. "He's blond, too."

Smiling, he didn't trouble to set her straight.

It's cozy to imagine the three of us as a family, Laura admitted. And difficult to believe we won't see him again for years, if ever again, though we met for the first time yesterday. She supposed she hadn't known what she was missing as a single mother, because she'd never been anything else. Guy had died before the two of them could be parents together.

From what Guy had told her, Enzo had been a bachelor at age thirty-four. For some reason, she'd simply assumed that was still the case. But what if it wasn't? To her chagrin, Laura found she didn't like the notion of a wife waiting back in Italy for him.

"Are you married? Divorced? Do you have any children?" she blurted before propriety and embarrassment could stifle her questions.

Something sad and a little wary flickered in the dark eyes that so resembled those of her sixteenth-century courtier. "I came close to getting married once," he said, continuing to watch Paolo rather than look at her. "We had a falling-out and went our separate ways. Having children is something I've greatly missed."

When they returned to the apartment an hour or so later, Laura wasn't eager for him to go. "If you're not in too much of a hurry, perhaps you have time for a cup of coffee," she suggested.

Accepting, he remarked that he'd like to go through her photo album again. She invited him to help himself from the bookcase while she set up the coffeepot and put Paolo down for a nap. His prized sailboat propped against the lamp on the night table beside his bed, Paolo shut his eyes readily enough. Carrying the coffee into the living room on a tray, Laura joined Enzo on the couch. They sipped in silence for a few moments as he turned the album's pages.

"These pictures are priceless, Laura," he said at last, turning to her. "Would you mind very much copying some of them for my mother? I'll gladly reimburse you for the expense."

To Laura's knowledge, during the years Guy had spent in America, Anna Rossi had been the only member of his immediate family to stay in touch with him. "I'd be happy to," she replied, "so long as you don't insist on paying for them."

"Thanks. I appreciate it." Taking out his billfold, he handed her his business card so that she could send the photos to his business address.

A small silence ensued, one in which she sensed he had further questions.

"Is the city a good place to raise children?" he asked after a moment, confirming her speculation. "Where will Paolo go to school when he's old enough?"

It wasn't the sort of query she'd expected, and Laura took a moment to compose herself before answering it. "Probably not here in Chicago," she said at last.

He quirked one brow.

"My partner, Carol Merchant, and I are thinking of moving Rossi Originals to New York, in order to be closer to the heart of the garment business," she explained. "I know it won't be the country, with cows, chickens and fresh air. But it's a very cosmopolitan city. I'm convinced I can make a good life for him there. When he's old enough, I plan to send him to private school."

Quietly Enzo appraised her. "Forgive me if I'm being too inquisitive. But from what you told me, your design business is still in its infancy. Will you be able to afford it?"

About to tell him her finances were none of his affair, that she'd managed for four years without the Rossis' interference or help, Laura bit back her retort. Enough harsh words had been spoken in his family already.

"As a matter of fact, I can," she told him, "thanks to Guy's inheritance from his grandmother and the money the race car manufacturer's insurance company paid us after the faulty steering column that caused your brother's crash was discovered. I used the former to start my business, and put the latter into tax-free bonds for Paolo's education."

Again there was silence, and Laura found herself wishing she could read her dark-eyed companion's thoughts. Did he think she'd managed well? Or had he found room to criticize?

"Our trip to the zoo this morning pleased me very much, and I was wondering... May I return to visit you next week, before flying back to Italy?'' he asked, surprising her by going off on a different tack altogether.

Strongly attracted to him, though she believed nothing more intimate than a brother-sister relationship would ever develop between them, Laura suppressed a rush of elation. They'd see each other again! "Of course you may," she answered, trying not to let the extent of her enthusiasm show. "Paolo and I have thoroughly enjoyed your visit."

As the workweek began in Rossi Originals' sketch-and-fabric-sample-cluttered atelier overlooking Wabash Avenue, Laura couldn't get her husband's brother out of her thoughts. The fact that he hadn't pressed her to help him heal the breach in his family, but instead had left the subject unresolved, was prompting her to reconsider doing as he'd asked.

Maybe we *should* go while Paolo's still preschool-age and it's easier to get away, she thought Wednesday afternoon, chewing distractedly on her drawing pencil as she stared into space at her drafting table. If Enzo's serious about paying our expenses, it wouldn't cost us anything. Forget Umberto and the way he acted. My son has a right to know his heritage. . . .

"A penny for your thoughts," Carol offered, entering her work area with a sheaf of invoices under her arm as the city's famous El train rattled by outside the windows. "You've been doing more woolgathering than designing this afternoon."

Laura rolled her eyes. "Sorry. I realize I've been a bit preoccupied the past few days."

"I don't suppose it has anything to do with your handsome brother-in-law and the fact that he's returning tomorrow afternoon."

As usual, her friend and partner was close to the mark. Laura couldn't deny she'd been obsessed with Enzo since meeting him. Or deny his good looks. She'd made the mistake of showing Carol the photograph of him with his arm about Guy's shoulders. However, she *hadn't* told the fifty-year-old former schoolteacher about the dizzy spells she'd suffered while viewing the Renaissance nobleman's portrait. Or her feeling that there was some sort of connection between it and her unexpected visitor.

Murmuring that perhaps she needed to talk, Laura suggested they brew themselves some fresh coffee and take a break. It wasn't long before the whole story of her fragmentary visions had come tumbling out, along with her strong impression that Enzo resembled the man in the portrait.

"It's not his features, exactly," she related. "It's his eyes. They're dark, like those of the sixteenth-century courtier. And they have the same expression. You'd swear they're thinking the same thoughts. I almost jumped out of my skin when he turned up on my doorstep after the second incident."

Carol shook her head. "I don't know what to tell you. I haven't met your brother-in-law. Or seen the portrait. As for the sensations that accompanied your dizziness... They could have resulted from fatigue. Skipping meals. Or the antihistamine you took. Overwork would be my guess. I know we've got a lot to do, especially if we're going to move to New York next spring. But we're in the black for the first time since we hung out our shingle. You could afford to take time off. Slow down a bit."

Laura leaned her chin on one hand, unconsciously imitating a sketch pinned to the bulletin board behind her. "That's what Enzo wants me to do," she said. "He..."

Her attention focused on a single area of concern, Carol didn't appear to be listening. "I do think that, if the spells return, you ought to see a doctor," she advised.

As the one who'd experienced them, Laura didn't think her dizzy spells presaged a serious illness. "I will, of course," she promised. "But since the incidents happened at the Art Institute, and I don't plan to return there until the Renaissance show is over, I doubt I'll be troubled by them again."

In answer, Carol gave her a look that said, "Who can tell?"

"Not to change the subject, but did you mean it about my taking time off?" Laura added. "Enzo has offered to pay our way to Italy so Paolo can meet his grandparents. Though their father treated Guy abominably, he's sick now. Supposedly he wants to make amends."

"Laura, how wonderful!" Her partner's sturdy, clean-scrubbed face lit with enthusiasm. "I've always felt by-gones should be bygones in that situation—that Paolo should get to know his father's family," she emphasized. "Besides, you haven't taken a vacation since giving birth. This sounds like the perfect opportunity. The business can get along without you for a couple of weeks."

That night, after Paolo was asleep, Laura got out her fa-vorite photo of her late husband. She'd taken it on the Yorkshire moors when they'd gone to England so that he could race at Silverstone. In it, the breeze had ruffled his blond hair. A lighter brown than Enzo's with glints of ha-zel in them, his eyes had been looking lovingly at her when she snapped the shutter.

"What do you think, Guy?" she asked pensively. "Should we accept Enzo's proposal? Or would you prefer that we don't reopen the dialogue with your family?"

As always when she sought Guy's advice, the answer was silence. She'd have to decide without his help. She was still mulling it over the following afternoon as she paused on her way from the bus stop to her apartment to purchase a bouquet of daisies from a sidewalk vendor.

She'd come within a block of her doorstep when a deep, charmingly accented voice called her name, followed by the sound of light, rapid footsteps.

It was Enzo. He hadn't fastened his tie, and it blew back over his shoulder as he hurried to catch up with her. His suit was creased as if he'd just gotten off the plane, and his hair was slightly mussed, giving him a casual look. She noted stray golden glints in it.

"Hello!" he said, taking her arm and smiling down at her. "Small world, isn't it, that we meet on a Chicago street this way? Since I'll just be staying overnight this trip, I didn't rent a car. I decided to walk from my hotel."

She could feel her own smile spreading like molasses independent of any direction from her. It was so good to see him. "It's a perfect day for it," she answered. "How was Detroit? Did your negotiations work out?"

"It's a bit early to tell. But, yes, I think so."

They were standing like a two-person island in a river of pedestrians, he in his wrinkled suit, she in a sleeveless cotton dress of her own design, printed with daisies and bachelor's buttons. A second conversation that had nothing to do with words was going on between them.

She's so fresh-looking, so gamine, he thought, gazing down at her. And, above all, so hauntingly familiar. It's as if I knew her before we met. That snapshot Guy showed me in Florida can't begin to account for it.

"Laura," he murmured, acting on a hunch born of the receptivity he sensed in her big green eyes, "forgive me if I speak of it the moment we meet. But I can't help wondering. Have you changed your mind about traveling to Italy so Paolo can meet my parents? Something in your face..."

As the words tumbled out, she could feel the weight of her decision settling into place. "As a matter of fact, I have," she said, flinging whatever misgivings she still held to the four winds. "Like you, I want Paolo to know his father's family. I thought perhaps two or three weeks..."

"But that's wonderful!" he exclaimed.

Before Laura knew what was happening, Enzo had snatched her by the waist and danced her around in a circle. A policeman gave them an indulgent look.

For the first time since he and Laura had met, the smile that warmed Enzo's mouth and eyes seemed to emanate fully from his deepest self. She felt as if she'd been handed a benediction. "I'm delighted that you're pleased," she said. "Because in some ways I feel as if I'm stepping off a cliff, doing this."

Her residual hesitation didn't seem to translate. "Are you packed yet?" he demanded, his hand lightly gripping her arm as he propelled her along the sidewalk. "My ticket's for tomorrow morning. Since we'll be traveling first-class, it shouldn't be too difficult to reserve the extra seats."

It hadn't occurred to her that he'd expect her to accompany him right away. Surely, as a businessman, he realized she couldn't pick up and leave her fashion-design firm without advance preparation.

"Hold on half a minute," she protested. "I just made up my mind. I doubt we can be ready that soon."

Her assent in his grasp, Enzo wasn't about to hand it back in increments. "Of course you can," he insisted. "There's no time like the present. Besides, it makes sense for you and Paolo to travel with me. I'll be able to watch over you that way."

The idea of Enzo acting as their guardian angel caused a warm little glow to expand in the pit of Laura's stomach. I wonder what it would be like, she thought, simply to relax into his keeping?

Meanwhile, the steamroller of his will had been slowed to a crawl by practicality. "You do have passports?" he asked, anxiously drawing his dark brows together.

The dimple that flashed beside her mouth quickly laid his concern to rest. "I got mine when Guy and I traveled to England six years ago," she told him. "It's still valid. As for Paolo's, I applied for it when he was a year old, thinking we might accompany my parents on a dig in Mexico."

He gave her hand a little squeeze. "*Molto bene!* Then we're all set."

They'd arrived at her doorstep and, with a little gesture, he motioned her to precede him up the stairs. Her head spinning at the rapid turn of events, Laura told an astonished Josie they'd be going to Italy and arranged for her to pick up the mail and come in periodically to water the plants. While Enzo dialed the airline, she sat Paolo down and explained the trip to him.

His eyes saucer-wide, her son didn't fully comprehend. "Will we be gone more than a day, Mommy?" he asked. "Can I take my race cars? And my new sailboat?"

Still on the phone, Enzo gave a thumbs-up signal to indicate that his quest for tickets had been successful. I'll have to call Carol, Laura though' dazedly as he got out his credit card and read off the number and expiration date. She doubted her friend and partner had envisioned such an abrupt leave-taking when she'd given the proposed trip her blessing.

Their departure was to be even more abrupt than Laura had expected. When he got off the phone, Enzo broke the news that they'd be taking off for Milan that evening, instead. "I hope it's all right. The connections were better that way," he explained apologetically.

From Laura's point of view, things were moving too fast for comfort. Yet what was she supposed to do? Insist they delay for eight hours? Aside from giving her additional time to pack, she couldn't see what that would accomplish.

Swept along by a river she sensed was much broader and deeper than Enzo's enthusiasm and her own acquiescence to his wishes, she called Carol and filled her in on their plans. Her partner's reaction skidded from shock through swift calculation to encouragement.

"Have fun," Carol instructed as they said goodbye. "And for heaven's sake, don't worry. Two and a half weeks isn't a very long time. If a crisis erupts, I can handle it."

At Laura's request, Enzo watched television with her son and supervised his consumption of a TV dinner while she packed. Selecting items from her closet and Paolo's with as much foresight as she could muster, she all but threw them into the set of matched suitcases Guy had given her for her twenty-eighth birthday. At the last moment, she tossed in the photo album, her sketchbook and her favorite picture of Guy for good measure. I hope we're doing the right thing, she thought.

They were ready to leave at a quarter past eight. Summoning a taxi, Enzo directed the driver to his hotel and asked him to wait while he ran inside to collect his luggage and pay the bill. Within minutes, they were hurtling past the Kennedy Expressway's glare of lights on their way to O'Hare International Airport.

They'd left Paolo's sailboat at home and, to compensate, Enzo bought him a model airliner at the terminal. "You'll spoil him," Laura protested over her son's delight as they headed for their assigned gate.

Enzo threw her one of his stubborn, dark-eyed glances. "No more than I spoil myself," he insisted. "Besides, I gave him the plane for a very practical reason. Playing with it will help to ease any fears he might have about taking off on his first flight."

Buckled into a window seat, with Laura next to him and Enzo across the aisle, Paolo was agog at the way buildings seemed to shrink as their plane gained altitude. His nose pressed to the cabin window, he forgot to swoop and swirl his toy in the air as he gazed at the city's glittering panoply of lights. Later, though he picked with little apparent hunger at the snack the stewardess served, he seemed enchanted by the tray and the little cups.

By the time they landed at Kennedy, he was sleepy, and he napped on Laura's lap in the VIP lounge as they waited for their Milan flight. Pausing at a newsstand, Enzo had managed to purchase a day-old copy of *La Stampa*, his hometown newspaper. He sat quietly at her side, the sleeve of his suit jacket occasionally brushing hers as he read it and scanned the stock quotations.

From her perspective, their trip had an air of unreality about it. She felt as if she could pinch herself and the terminal would disappear. Yet, at the same time, it seemed the inevitable outcome of her surrender to a fate that had always lain in store. Like the elderly woman at the zoo, she realized, their fellow occupants of the lounge probably viewed her and Enzo as a couple. She got the impression the solitary blonde seated across from them envied her.

Their new seating arrangements proved similar to those on their flight from Chicago. His routine upset, Paolo was cranky when they got on board, and soothing him demanded her full attention. However, once they'd left the city lights behind and started their journey across the dark, trackless expanse of the Atlantic, his eyes began to close.

"Excuse me, *signora*," a pleasant, raven-haired stewardess said, leaning over them. "But the cabin isn't crowded. And we aren't experiencing much turbulence. If you'd like to sit across the aisle with your husband, your son could stretch out across two seats with a pillow and blanket."

Their eyes meeting in acknowledgment of the stewardess's error, Laura and Enzo exchanged a glance that, for her at least, was charged with the electric current of their first meeting. He feels it, too, she thought, as a muscle tightened in his jaw. I know he does. A moment later, she decided she'd imagined it.

"I suppose it would be all right," she said, unbuckling her seat belt and getting to her feet in order to help the stewardess make her child comfortable.

When Paolo's eyes had drifted shut once more, Enzo stood to offer her the vacant place beside him, next to the window. Simultaneously someone turned off the cabin's overhead lights. As they relaxed in their cushiony seats, he spoke softly to Laura of his childhood with Guy, and some of the sights he'd show them at their destination.

After a while, lulled by his voice and the monotonous hum of the plane's engines, she got sleepy, too. The thread of his conversation eluded her. She was fully asleep, her breath coming softly and evenly, when her head sank onto Enzo's shoulder.

Their stewardess was nowhere in sight. Unobserved by Laura's sleeping son and the sprinkling of other passengers who shared the first-class cabin with them, Enzo smoothed a strand of her hair back from her face. It was shiny and soft, yet springy to the touch—and subtly erotic to his senses. While he lived, my brother was a lucky man, he thought as he, too, shut his eyes. He doubted he'd ever be so fortunate.

Chapter Three

Somewhere over the Atlantic, as they crossed a time zone empty of human habitation, Laura awoke to find her cheek pillowed on subtly textured raw silk with solid male muscle beneath it. She experienced warmth, an unaccustomed yet hauntingly familiar sense of having someone to look after her. The elusive aroma of a citrus-based after-shave, faded but still discernible many hours after its application, tantalized her nostrils.

In her sleep, it seemed, she'd sought Enzo as a woman seeks her mate beneath the bed covers, for security and comfort. She knew at once, without having to be told, that he'd remained wakeful. At some point during his vigil, she realized, he or the stewardess had tucked a monogrammed airline blanket about her shoulders.

"Sorry," she whispered, stifling a yawn as she sat up and rubbed away traces of smudged mascara. "I hope I didn't keep you awake, leaning on you."

Though his arm prickled from lack of circulation and he longed to flex his shoulder, Enzo half regretted the necessity of relinquishing his burden. It had seemed so cozy, so *right* somehow, resting his cheek against her hair and sustaining her as she slept.

He kept his response low, to avoid waking their fellow passengers. "You didn't. I don't usually sleep well on airplanes."

She glanced across the aisle. "Paolo..."

"He's fine. I've kept an eye on him."

Excusing herself, she got to her feet, adjusted her son's blanket and went to use the lavatory. When she returned, Enzo had retrieved pillows from the overhead bin for each of them. His hair was mussed, and his eyes were hollow with fatigue. As she brushed past him, she noticed that, in the hours since their departure from Chicago, he'd grown a shadow beard.

A bit self-consciously, she settled into her seat. "I didn't snore, did I?" she asked.

Despite his weariness, the laugh lines beside his mouth deepened. She was so American, so plainspoken. Even when she felt awkward or embarrassed, she went straight to the point. He imagined Guy had found that quality endearing and refreshing.

"Not really," he assured her with his best European gallantry. "The little sounds you made were actually quite restful."

She didn't respond, and, in the cabin's hushed, dimly lit ambience, they both managed to sleep a little. Their eyes opened sometime later, when Paolo tugged on Laura's sleeve to announce that the sun was up and their stewardess was serving breakfast.

They landed at Milan, a gleaming modern city in the shadow of snow-capped mountains, shortly after 10:00 a.m. local time. The terminal at busy Malpensa Airport, where

Enzo said most intercontinental flights serving the Lombard capital landed, hummed with a polyglot babble that was dominated by Italian. Repeated announcements in that language, followed by German, French, English and Spanish, assaulted their ears. Everyone in the terminal's crowded concourses seemed to be talking rapidly and gesturing expansively.

Out of his element, Paolo clung tightly to Laura's hand as Enzo shepherded them through customs. And, though she did her best to hide it from him, she felt some apprehension of her own. What will the Rossis think when we arrive on their doorstep? she asked herself. Of course, their visit wouldn't come as a complete surprise to Guy's mother and father, and the grandmother he'd claimed had always ruled the family with a iron hand. At Laura's urging, Enzo had wired them from Chicago. But he hadn't waited for a response before they got under way.

When it came to facing her as-yet-unknown in-laws, her only ally would be the dark-haired man who'd been her companion through the night and shaved in the lavatory just prior to their landing at Malpensa—a man she barely knew. Could she trust him to take her part against them if the need arose? Or would he abandon her to hostility and rejection? She sensed he was given to dark moods, withdrawal and occasional self-doubt, though at the moment he seemed reliable enough.

Their plane for Turin departed almost at once, and there wasn't time for second thoughts. The stewardesses and most of the passengers spoke Italian as a matter of course, and Laura found herself acclimating. She'd learned to speak the language from Guy, and already her fluency was returning.

Thanks to a cloudless sky and their more modest altitude on the brief intercity hop, she was able to see something of the countryside. Blue-white peaks shimmered in the distance to the north and west. She glimpsed patches of woods, tile-roofed farmhouses, the occasional castle, sunny hills given over to viticulture. Through it all, a river snaked like a ribbon of silver. The lakes were bluer than blue, scattered as if by a giant hand. Guy had described them as God's mirrors, poised to catch the vanity of paradise.

As they circled Turin for a landing, the apprehension she'd pushed down at Milan returned to plague her. Seated next to Paolo, she literally jumped when Enzo reached across the aisle to give her hand a gentle squeeze.

"We won't be going down to the country right away," he reassured her. "You and Paolo will want to freshen up and change at my apartment. And I'll need to attend to a few matters at the factory. While we're there, I thought you might like a tour."

They waited at the curb with their luggage while Enzo went to retrieve his white Rossi Falconetta convertible from the long-term parking lot. Though its trunk was so small as to be almost nonexistent, somehow he managed to load everything on board. To do it, he had to nestle several of their smaller bags beside Paolo in the abbreviated backseat and strap Laura's large cases to the rear-mounted luggage rack.

Turin proved to be a cosmopolitan, graceful city with glittering shops, beautifully manicured piazzas and elegant baroque palaces. On their way to his apartment, Enzo pointed out the Cathedral of San Giovanni with its famous Chapel of the Holy Shroud.

"Does it really look as if a face is imprinted on the cloth?" Laura asked.

He threw her an indulgent glance from behind dark glasses. "Before you return to Chicago, I'll take you to see it," he promised. "You can decide for yourself."

His apartment turned out to be situated on the third floor of a stone palazzo that functioned as the Rossis' city abode.

"I'm the only one who spends any time here, now that my father is unwell," he explained as a servant unloaded their belongings and carried them inside. "My sister Cristina and her husband, Vittorio, who acts as my second in command at the factory, have their own place a few blocks away. As for the rest of the family, both my grandmother and my mother prefer the country. Sofia . . ."

He shrugged at the mention of his older sister, who was divorced and childless. "When she's not at the Villa Voglia," he added, "she divides her time between Rome and San Remo, not to mention Paris and her other favorite watering holes."

To Laura, the Palazzo Rossi's vast foyer appeared coldly formal. An intimidating expanse of marble, mirrors and gilt, it was relieved only slightly by a scattering of murky portraits and a yellow-silk-paneled salon glimpsed through a partly open door.

As they ascended to the third floor in a small cage-style elevator that offered glimpses of an ornate second-floor hallway, she puzzled over Enzo's failure to allude to Stefano, his only remaining brother. Or rather his *half* brother, she corrected herself.

She couldn't help wondering if the omission stemmed from dislike, condescension and pity for Stefano, similar to that which Guy had expressed. Did the brothers' negative view of him originate with the fact that his mother was one of Umberto Rossi's lower-class mistresses from the Turin slums? Surely they didn't look down on him because he had the added misfortune of having been born with a clubfoot.

As much as she'd loved Guy, Laura had never approved of his attitude toward Stefano, who hadn't chosen his parentage. She began to feel a twinge of sympathy for the family interloper.

Unlike the stiffly formal air of the Palazzo Rossi's lower floors, Enzo's apartment was charming and decidedly unstuffy to Laura's artistic eye. Anything but bland, despite its off-white walls and upholstered furniture, the sitting room boasted a nineteenth-century ushak rug woven in cream, bittersweet and celery, with matching silk pillows.

A double footstool with spool-turned legs was covered in a wool tapestry zebraskin print. Crowned by valances finished in jagged points, the drapes that ornamented a row of tall, narrow windows overlooking the street were fashioned of heavy topaz velvet. She suspected the walnut bookcase inlaid with antique Florentine *pietra dura* panels was priceless.

But it was Enzo's choice in art that whispered of the man's taste and caused her to realize fully for the first time what caliber of wealth Guy had renounced in order to be his own person. Hobnobbing casually over a sectional sofa were a Dubuffet gouache, a glowing Frank Stella abstract and several Picasso lithographs. In one corner, a muscular Henry Moore bronze exuded the power of the physical atop its walnut plinth. In another, three scarred and time-bleached wooden saints she imagined had been salvaged from a crumbling church formed an eclectic, almost conversational grouping.

"Enzo, your art collection... *è magnifico!*" she exclaimed, unconsciously delivering part of the accolade in his native tongue.

He didn't fail to notice the slip. It's as if she belongs here, he thought. As if this room has just been waiting for her to walk in and appreciate it.

A moment later, he was cautioning himself not to invest too much of himself in the situation. She was his sister-in-law, the widow of his dead brother. She wouldn't be staying in Italy long. If those arguments don't put a crimp in your interest, he reflected, try a few others you could name. You don't want to wish your bad dreams and moodiness on a woman like her.

"I'm glad you like it," he answered, the pleasure his smile betrayed warring with the touch of melancholy that shadowed his gaze. "Come, I'll show you to one of my guest bedrooms, where you and Paolo can bathe and change."

After they'd showered and put on fresh clothing—short pants and a T-shirt for Paolo, a soft rose sweater and printed silk skirt from a former Rossi Originals collection for Laura—Enzo took them to lunch at one of his favorite *caffès,* the brocade-and-gilt-bedecked Torino, on the Piazza San Carlo.

"It is the city's oldest, the most authentic," he related as a waiter showed them to a table by the windows. Spread with a lace-bordered tablecloth, it overlooked an imposing square flanked by porticoed shops and restaurants finished in cream-colored stucco with rhythmic rows of gray shutters.

According to Enzo, who directed Laura's gaze to a trio of dowagers gossiping over a hearty lunch and a handful of solitary, nattily dressed old men consuming tea and pastries as they read their newspapers, the cafe's clientele was mostly "old Turin," amiable, self-satisfied and well-heeled.

"Hard to believe, isn't it," he mused, "that this city has a split personality? It's the second richest in Italy...and the home of the labor-union movement, as well as the Red Brigades, which espoused the Communist movement. You'll see the contrast more clearly when we travel south to the factory. Many of Turin's auto workers live in what can only be termed a giant slum. As exclusively luxury, sport and race car manufacturers these days, we pay better-than-average wages. But we're just a small part of the local economy, I'm afraid."

When they'd finished their green salad and fondue with white truffles, and Paolo had polished off a dish of *agnolotti* and a miniature molded chocolate cream, Enzo took them to visit Rossi Motorworks. Compared with the huge Fiat plant, he told Laura, the establishment was relatively small.

As he'd warned, they had to traverse a depressing urban sprawl to reach its front gate.

Entering through a square-cut opening in the center of a rusty redbrick 1920's-vintage factory building, they entered a broad interior courtyard striped with numbered parking spaces for VIPs and visitors. Atop a tall pole, a flag displaying the Rossi logo, a lion rampant on a field of blue with a coronet floating above its head, fluttered in the breeze.

With a little flourish, Enzo downshifted and parked beside the steel-and-glass entry to an adjoining five-story modern industrial complex. "Museum first?" he inquired with a grin, throwing Paolo a look. "Or the production line where they make the race cars?"

The boy was agog. "The place where they make the race cars, *please!*" he begged.

They started in the design shop, where a half-dozen engineers in dress pants, shirts and ties bent over drafting tables. "This is how a brand-new car begins, with a drawing," Enzo explained to his towheaded nephew. "It must be done very carefully, with all the measurements just right, so that when the car is built it will fit perfectly together."

"Did you ever design a car?" Paolo asked.

Enzo nodded. "I have helped design one. My father made sure I tried my hand at every job in the factory, including hand-rubbing finishes and installing exhaust systems, before he let me take over in his place."

Proceeding to the huge open assembly area, with its massive overhead steel beams and color-coded automated transfer line, they watched doors being attached, engines being assembled, bodies being painted. To Laura, though the finely wrought Italian machine tools that carried out some of the more toxic operations, such as rustproofing, were run by American-made computers, the amount of manual labor that went into the latest Rossi Francetta racers was phenomenal. Everywhere she looked, it seemed, blue-uniformed workmen were fitting upholstery, wiring spaceship-worthy dashboards and correcting minor body flaws with the exquisite attention to detail of Michelangelo putting the finishing touches on his *David*.

Not too surprisingly, Paolo liked the foundry where the Rossi engine blocks were cast. Pouring specially blended alloys into red-hot cauldrons of silvery molten metal, the gloved, goggled and hard-hatted molders stirred their witches' brews with long paddles, stepping back only slightly when the mixture ignited and flashed with the brilliance of red-orange hellfire.

Paolo positively loved sitting behind the wheel of a low-slung red experimental model with gull-wing doors Enzo told him had been dubbed *Il Predatore*. "Someday," he told his mother with a determined gleam in his eyes, "I'll drive a car like this one."

Enzo ruffled his hair. "Someday you'll design one."

On their way to view the Level I test track, which was situated at the rear of the factory property, Enzo talked of four-valve cylinder heads, the sizes of engines. Though his words were mostly incomprehensible to Laura, Paolo listened to them with a rapt attention that suggested he'd been waiting all his life to hear them. Though he was only four, she doubted he'd ever get enough of "gaited upshifts" and "cornering power."

The family passion for cars and speed is in his blood, she thought. Guy bequeathed it to him. Given half a chance, Enzo would cultivate it.

Their tour was cut short a few minutes later when they stopped at Enzo's office on their way to the motorworks museum. Sighting them, his secretary jumped to her feet. "Signor Rossi... your grandmother's been trying to reach you!" she exclaimed. "It's your father. He's had another stroke."

Oh, no! I hope our impending arrival didn't trigger it! Laura thought in dismay, drawing Paolo close and warning him to behave.

His face darkening, Enzo picked up a phone and stabbed out a phone number. His conversation with his paternal grandmother, eighty-seven-year-old Emilia da Sforza Rossi, was brief. "I don't think the situation is critical," he announced in response to Laura's worried look when he put down the receiver. "As I told you the day we met, he's had these little cerebral accidents before. But there isn't any question that, each time they occur, they weaken him. We'd better get down to the country right away."

They returned to the Palazzo Rossi to collect their luggage, and they were quickly on their way. Though their mood was somber, the top was down on Enzo's convertible as they left Turin behind, and the weather was bright and breezy. Cheerful and impersonal, the sun warmed their faces.

Before long, they were passing farmhouses, woods and little streams. The vine-covered hills that surrounded them resembled those Laura had seen from the plane. To Paolo's delight, they passed a medieval castle perched high on a promontory. Though its walls were in bad repair, and birds probably nested in its ravaged turrets, it remained imposing.

"Did knights and dragons live there, Mommy?" Paolo asked.

"I don't think the dragons did, darling," she said, her hair whipping in her face as she turned to look at him. "They weren't exactly pets."

His eyes hidden behind dark glasses, Enzo concentrated on the road ahead. Now and then he massaged the bridge of his nose, as if he were getting a headache. The closer they came to the Rossi country home, it seemed, the more forbidding his mood became.

It's only natural for him to worry, Laura tried to tell her-self. His father's life is on the line. Yet she couldn't shrug off a sense that Umberto's illness wasn't the only thing trou-bling Enzo. Is it the impending contact with his family that's causing him to withdraw into himself? she wondered. Or something about the house itself that arouses negative emotions?

Her own nervousness about meeting the Rossis, particu-larly at a moment of family crisis, rose perceptibly as they turned off the secondary route they'd been traveling since leaving the S-10 and headed up a private avenue flanked by cypresses. But it was nothing to the uneasiness she felt when the Villa Voglia came into view.

More Florentine than Turinese, the Rossis' country home was a classically proportioned gem of Renaissance archi-tecture. Fashioned of faded pink stucco trimmed with creamy stone, it had a terra-cotta barrel-tile roof and ab-breviated, evenly balanced wings, a second-floor balcony across the center section, and a ground-floor colonnade of arches that probably provided ventilation for the base-ment.

Twin flights of stone steps ascended to a broad stone ter-race. The columned formal entrance was flanked by sym-metrically placed floor-to-ceiling windows.

There was also a watchtower, or "dovecote," as Laura's late husband had called it. He hadn't prepared her for the Villa Voglia's beauty. Or the way the fountain at the center of its formal garden stirred remembered images. Lots of Italian country homes have fountains, her practical self in-sisted. There can't be any connection—either to that dream I had, or to the fact that Enzo brought me here. So why do they seem related?

Enzo stopped the car at the foot of one of the twin stair-cases, and, as at Palazzo Rossi, a servant appeared to col-lect their luggage. He was followed by a thin, dark-haired young woman of great beauty, who didn't descend to meet them, but instead remained on the terrace, leaning over the balustrade.

"So you're here at last." She addressed Enzo in rapid Italian without acknowledging Laura's or Paolo's presence. "The doctor's with him now. Grandmother said you're to go up the moment you arrive."

Concerned though he obviously was, Enzo didn't neglect his manners. "Laura, this is my sister Cristina," he responded in English, making amends for his sibling's gaffe, as they mounted the steps. "Cristina, I'd like you to meet your sister-in-law, Laura Rossi, and her son, Paolo, from America. Perhaps while I'm with Father you could make them welcome...ask Gemma to show them to their rooms."

The unspoken reprimand clearly wasn't lost on her. "How do you do?" she murmured, following his lead and switching to heavily accented English. Her smile was a little forced. "Would you like something to eat? Or perhaps, after your long journey, you'd prefer to rest?"

After their lunch at the Caffè Torino, they were anything but famished. But Laura knew Paolo could use a nap. For her part, she wanted a few minutes alone, to put the events of the past few days, as well as her baffling familiarity with the villa's garden and its central fountain, into better perspective. I'd much rather meet the rest of the family later, with Enzo at my side to run interference, she thought.

"I'm happy to make your acquaintance at last, Cristina," she responded, with a small, uncertain smile of her own. "As for your suggestion, a rest would be lovely. I hope our presence here just now won't prove too unsettling."

Though she nodded, Cristina didn't voice an opinion, and the four of them went into the house together, passing through a partially open loggia into a formal but charming *sala* with faded frescoes visible beneath its nineteenth-century paintings. The floor was black-and-white marble.

A concave molding ornamented with putti in whimsical poses bordered the coffered ceiling.

Identical flights of stairs ascended to the second floor from either side of the room. Resting a hand on the gilt-trimmed newel post of the one on the left, Enzo apologized for having to leave Laura for the moment. "We'll be reunited this evening at the dinner table," he promised. "I'll introduce you to everyone then."

To her, the mask of tension that had descended over his features caused him to resemble the stranger he'd been just a week earlier. It also made him look like the courtier in the Art Institute painting. "We'll be fine," she responded, with a bit more confidence than she felt. "Please don't worry about us. Right now, your father needs your undivided attention."

Giving her a grateful look, he took the stairs at a brisk pace. As Cristina rang for the maid, Laura spied an overweight, unpleasant-looking boy of about eight who was watching them through the partially open doorway of a side room.

"My son, Bernardo," Cristina supplied shortly, bypassing an actual introduction. "Ah... here's Gemma now. Under the circumstances, I'm sure you'll understand if I place you in her care and return to my father's side."

Laura answered in the affirmative, relieved at the chance to collect her thoughts. Taking Paolo's hand, she accompanied the friendly young maid upstairs to the rooms that had been assigned to them. To her discomfort, with each step she took, her sense of déjà vu increased. Yet nothing about the villa's second floor, which was given over to bedrooms and sitting rooms, appeared the least familiar to her.

It's because Guy described the house to me, she reassured herself. I feel I know it for that reason.

When they entered the high-ceilinged sitting room that separated her bedroom from the one Paolo would occupy, however, she knew that wasn't the case. Almost immediately, her ears began to buzz. With the suddenness of an avalanche, the light-headedness and blurring of lights and colors she'd experienced in front of the Renaissance nobleman's portrait assailed her.

No! she vowed, catching hold of a fringed, velvet-upholstered armchair to steady herself. I won't let this happen. There has to be a rational explanation. She couldn't guess how pale she'd become. Or how unsteady she suddenly appeared.

Paolo was watching her with a frightened look. "Mommy?" he asked in a quavery voice.

"Is anything wrong, *signora?*" Gemma echoed, an expression of grave concern coming over her face.

Somehow Laura managed to push down her vertigo, to deny whatever force was fragmenting her experience and causing her to hallucinate. "Nothing a nap won't cure," she answered determinedly, straightening her spine and willing her equilibrium to cooperate. "We've been running on borrowed energy since leaving Chicago. Perhaps we could unpack later. I'd like to put my son to bed...lie down for a little while myself."

Though the maid clearly wasn't convinced she should leave the American *signora* alone, she departed with a submissive little nod of her head. I should have seen a doctor, the way Carol suggested, Laura reproached herself as she helped Paolo remove his shoes and crawl beneath the embroidered coverlet in his connecting room. If nothing physical had turned up, at least I'd have known this nonsense was just my imagination.

Stubborn and intuitive, a little voice inside her head argued that her family physician would have given her a clean bill of health. And that it wouldn't have solved anything. Episodes like the one she'd just experienced would have continued unabated.

They're related to the painting of the sixteenth-century courtier in the Art Institute, and to this house, it whispered—and to Enzo, if you're willing to face the truth. If you stay and allow yourself to become more closely associated with him, their frequency will only escalate.

Chapter Four

As Laura sought the security of a nap in a sunny guest room overlooking the Villa Voglia's formal garden and cypress-lined drive, Enzo stood beside his father's heavy Genoese four-poster, gazing somberly at its ashen, shrunken inhabitant. Now that the Turin heart specialist who served as Umberto's personal physician had gone, the older man was dozing. His breathing was noisy, ragged, even a little uncouth. Looking at him now, it was difficult to believe he had once been a forceful, leonine figure bursting with energy, one who had moved with ease among wealthy industrialists, loved a series of mistresses, and caused more than his share of heartbreak.

Much as he wanted to accept it, Enzo couldn't keep from questioning the doctor's pronouncement that his father's latest episode hadn't been especially severe. It had left him exhausted, with his mouth dragging even more at one corner and a marked weakness in his left arm, hadn't it? As he stood there, his relief that the attack hadn't been fatal or necessitated Umberto's removal to a hospital was tempered by heightened awareness that the older man's days were numbered—running out like the sand in an hourglass. He could see their downhill trajectory very clearly, thanks to the perspective he'd gained from a week away, in the States.

Thank God I was able to persuade Laura to come to Italy with me and bring Paolo, he thought. Or rather that she was caring enough to persuade herself. If all went well, he believed, the falling-out with Guy, which he knew was eating at his father's gut, would be healed—insofar as that was possible. There'd be a reconciliation before it was too late.

As she sometimes did, his grandmother seemed to sense the direction his thoughts were taking. "So the child is here," she observed in her dry, authoritative way, making no reference to Laura's presence.

With her carefully coiffed iron-gray hair and the upright way she carried herself in her black silk dress, Enzo acknowledged, she looked far younger than her eighty-seven years. Yet, like her slowly dying son, she grew increasingly frail each time he looked at her. He hated to think of losing them both.

"Your great-grandson and his mother are resting," he replied, keeping his voice low.

The Rossi matriarch nodded with satisfaction.

Though she remained in the background, as usual, adding nothing to the interchange, Enzo caught his mother's ghost of a smile. She'll be the one to nurture Paolo while he's here, he realized. The one to whom, when Laura isn't available, he'll turn for comfort. Grandmother, on the other hand, will see him as part of her legacy to the Rossi family, a tool to carry out her will. If we let her, she'll take charge of him, begin grooming him to meet her expectations.

Having reluctantly accompanied Umberto's physician downstairs to his car at Enzo's request, Cristina returned to the sickroom as he asked whether there had been any emotional crises in the household during his absence.

She chose to take the query personally. "'Nardo hasn't done anything to upset Father, and neither have I, if that's what you're hinting," she shot back accusingly. "The fault is yours, for bringing that woman and her son here! How could you fail to realize it would only rekindle the pain of what happened eight years ago?"

Aware his sister's hostility sprang from a fear that her son's inheritance would suffer if Paolo was accepted into the family circle, Enzo dismissed her words with a glance.

"Father didn't object to their coming, did he?" he demanded, putting the question to Emilia, who would know best.

"On the contrary, he was pleased," the Rossi matriarch related, giving Cristina a forbidding look.

Laura's room was pink with the glow of sunset by the time Gemma woke her in order to summon her to the evening meal. The maid had already washed Paolo's face and combed his hair. Thanks to her, apparently, he was wearing his second fresh outfit since they'd left Chicago, a clean polo shirt and shorts. "Would you like me to iron something for you, *signora?*" she asked.

Before Laura could answer Paolo piped up with the news—gleaned from Gemma, no doubt—that the rest of the family was already seated at the dinner table.

Oh, no, she thought. Tardy for our first appearance. Nothing like getting off on the right foot.

"That won't be necessary," she said quickly, thinking with gratitude of the peach silk packable coordinates she'd designed herself and tossed in her suitcase for just such a contingency. "Sit here on my bed, Paolo, and play with your airplane, while Mommy dashes into the bathroom to change her clothes."

Except for Enzo's and Cristina's, none of the faces that greeted them as they walked into the villa's frescoed, lace-curtained dining room a few minutes later were familiar to her. Though she still was a bit groggy from her nap, she sensed diverse emotional undercurrents as Enzo stood and held out the chair next to his at the long refectory-style table.

"*Grazie,*" she whispered, taking refuge from the intensity of his dark gaze by looking down at the Venetian-lace tablecloth.

"*Prego.*" He gave her a little smile of encouragement. "Grandmother, Mother, Sofia, Vittorio, permit me to introduce Guy's widow, Laura. And their son, Paolo. I'm sure, like me, you're happy to have them with us at last."

As if by long custom, all eyes turned to Emilia, according her the privilege of speaking first.

"*Bene accetto,* Laura, Paolo," she murmured in a husky voice, adding in perfect if accented English, "welcome to the Villa Voglia. I trust this will be the first of many happy visits with us."

Like Enzo, Vittorio—Cristina's balding, sharp-featured husband—had gotten politely to his feet. "A pleasure to meet you," he echoed, his somewhat strained smile fading at his wife's daunting look.

Her figure ample, her dark blond hair carelessly combed back from her face, Enzo's older sister, Sofia, looked as easygoing and comfortable as an unmade bed. She barely glanced at Paolo, apparently having no interest in children. "Hello," she said casually as she nibbled on a piece of bread. "Enzo tells us you're a fashion designer. While you're here, you must take in the Milan collections."

From what Laura could tell, Enzo's faded, gentle-looking mother had long since resigned herself to living in Emilia's shadow. Yet, in her opinion, Anna's sweet smile and her soft, uncomplicated "Welcome" exerted the greatest appeal. Unlike her mother-in-law, whose dark eyes held a judgmental, yet almost acquisitive, glint, she appeared to offer unconditional love and acceptance.

With an alacrity that suggested she'd been asked to keep it warm against their arrival, the Rossi family cook brought in the main dish, a lamb roast with browned whole onions and fresh oregano. Subsequent trips to the kitchen produced green beans, tomatoes stuffed with herbs and bread crumbs, a magnificent risotto with peas and prosciutto and a delicate fricassee of mushrooms. There was also a mixed green salad, ready to be dressed with oil and vinegar from cruets nestled in a silver tray.

Despite the concern of those present for the sick man upstairs, a large bouquet of white spider mums mixed with yellow calendulas contributed to a festive atmosphere. The table service was about what Laura had expected—English china, French crystal, heavy sterling eating utensils that had probably been in the family for generations.

Enzo did the honors, opening several bottles of the Villa Voglia's own Barolo wine and carving up the roast. Gradually the conversation eased, became more voluble. Only Umberto, confined to his bed, and Stefano, charged with the day-to-day operation of the Villa Voglia, according to Guy, were missing from the family circle.

The latter joined them a few minutes later, his limp slight, thanks to an operation Laura had heard he'd undergone to correct his clubfoot in his eighteenth year. Smiling and, insofar as she could tell, insincerely apologetic, he made his grandmother a little bow. "Preparations for the grape harvest are going well," he reported, indirectly excusing himself for being late.

Turning toward Laura and giving her a level look, he added, "You must be my new sister-in-law."

A bit stiffly, as if he suspected Stefano of grandstanding, Enzo made the appropriate introductions.

Whatever resentment, if any, Umberto's illegitimate son felt toward Laura and Paolo for laying claim to yet another place above his in the family hierarchy, it didn't show. "Delighted to make your acquaintance," he said, giving her a wry, faintly twisted smile.

When he'd walked into the room, Laura had thought the resemblance between him and Enzo nothing short of remarkable. However, with a chance to study them a bit more closely, she found them to be quite dissimilar. Whereas Enzo was compact, muscular and intense, a man who exuded power as naturally as breathing, Stefano was deferential, lanky, a little stooped. She added the faded scar on his right cheek to her growing list of places and things she'd encountered in the past several weeks that were oddly familiar.

He has the demeanor of a hanger-on, she thought as he took a seat across the table from her. I suspect he both resents and tolerates his less-than-equal status as the price of acceptance. She didn't have the slightest doubt that there was bad blood between him and Enzo. The latter's animosity seemed to run far deeper than the mild dislike and condescension Guy had expressed.

As the meal progressed, the talk revolved around Laura's background, her education and her career as a fashion designer, with Emilia taking the lead in questioning her. The Rossi matriarch also asked about her parents and her lifestyle in the United States, giving her scant opportunity to do more than pick at her food. Unbending a little more when she turned to Paolo, Emilia asked him several questions, as well, then made an obvious attempt to conquer his shyness by regaling him with stories of his father's boyhood. He remained somewhat in awe of her, from what Laura could tell.

Guy's racing career and his rift with Umberto weren't mentioned. Though Enzo joined in the general conversation, as did Anna and Sofia, Cristina and Vittorio said little. Indulging a hearty appetite, which was probably the result of his active outdoor life, Stefano appeared to spend the bulk of his time watching Laura and gauging Enzo's interest in her.

Following dessert, a zuppa inglese that she announced for Laura's benefit had been assembled in the Florentine style, Emilia excused herself and returned to Umberto's room, waving aside an offer from Anna to accompany her.

Seeming to take the rebuff with equanimity, Anna suggested they have their coffee outdoors. "It's a beautiful night," she observed in her quiet way, "and quite warm, though there's a little breeze."

They settled in woven rush chairs on the villa's rear terrace, which overlooked the winery and grain storage buildings, shadowy woods and vine-clad hills. The moon was full, a flat-appearing disc that glowed like burnished silver.

"Il plenilunio più vicino all'equinozio d'autunno," Enzo quoted negligently. "Or as you say in English, the harvest moon."

Once Margherita, the Rossi's housekeeper-cook, had finished serving their coffee, Stefano took out a harmonica and played several jaunty tunes. Again Laura got the impression that the family Umberto had decreed must accept him was bent on keeping him at arm's length. She thought she could read antipathy in the frown that creased Enzo's brow whenever he looked at his half brother, and in Vittorio's and Cristina's marked inattention to his efforts. Only Anna—the least likely of the group to feel tolerance for her husband's love child, she'd have thought—appeared to treat him with kindness. Though he couldn't compare with Enzo, in her estimation, Laura began to feel a measure of sympathy for him.

A half hour later, it was time to put Paolo to bed. Despite his long nap, their transatlantic journey was beginning to tell on him. His left cheek was flushed from leaning against her knee as he sat beside her chair. Thick and dark in contrast to the green eyes he'd inherited from her, his long lashes were drooping.

Expressing gratitude for her in-laws' hospitality and bidding them good-night, Laura led her son upstairs. To ease the impact of their unfamiliar surroundings, she remained beside him for several minutes after helping him put on his pajamas and turning out the light.

We're so far from home, she thought. Though our return tickets are safely stashed in my purse, and it's a simple matter of boarding a plane to go home again, I have the most extraordinary sense of having burned our bridges, cast our lot.

She also had an irrational premonition of impending danger.

Get real, she reproached herself. You'll be home before you know it. Italy will seem far away then. You don't want to hurry things. *Or say goodbye to Enzo before you must,* a little voice whispered.

On the terrace, with Emilia absent in Umberto's room and Stefano absorbed by his playing, the man who'd spirited her halfway around the world had seemed more relaxed than he had at the dinner table. She'd felt their connection deepen perceptibly when he stood and put one arm around her for a moment as she rose from her chair, reminding her that he'd see her in the morning. Apparently he planned to take them on some kind of tour.

Something could develop between us, given half a chance, she acknowledged as she brushed a strand of hair back from Paolo's forehead, kissed him good-night and proceeded to her room. Stefano thinks so, too. I have a hunch he'd like to play the spoiler.

Seconds later, the seemingly mutual attraction between her and Enzo and the role his half brother might be poised to play in it were summarily banished from Laura's thoughts. As she started toward her rose-and-cream canopied bed, with its old-fashioned headboard lamps and pristine Pratesi linens, the by-now-familiar buzzing in her ears, the irresistible blurring of lights and colors, assailed her.

This time, the phenomenon was over almost before it had begun. Shaken and disoriented, she thought she heard a footstep behind her. Was it Enzo? Had he come upstairs for a private word?

Turning, she found herself staring at empty space. My mind is playing tricks on me, she thought. And no wonder, with these dizzy spells I'm having. The minute I get back to Chicago, I'm going to call my doctor for an appointment. There's nothing in this room to precipitate hallucinations. The problem must be physical.

Yet she was certain as she changed to her nightgown and got into bed that she'd heard something.

By morning, Umberto's condition had improved more than they'd had any right to hope. Over breakfast in a pleasant, sun-splashed room redolent of freshly brewed coffee, with the sound of church bells reaching them faintly through open French doors that led to the villa's rear terrace, Enzo related the news.

"He's asked to see you and Paolo," he told Laura, dabbing at one corner of his mouth with a hand-finished linen napkin. "I thought we might go up as soon as we've finished here, since he sleeps badly and tires well before noon."

Though she'd come to Italy for the express purpose of allowing Paolo and his Rossi grandfather to meet, she couldn't hide her hesitation. She hadn't expected the older man to be so sick. Or anticipated the depth of Cristina's antipathy toward them. She had the strong feeling Cristina blamed their arrival for her father's latest episode.

I don't want my son traumatized, she thought.

"Don't worry, *cara*," Enzo murmured as if she'd spoken, reaching across the table to squeeze her hand. "Paolo's a big boy. He can handle it. Besides, my father won't bite you *or* him."

So casually made, the gesture sent little prickles of pleasure skidding up her arm. Like the fact that he'd called her his "dear one," it gave her a warm, unsettled feeling. How handsome he is in that white shirt, open at the throat to reveal just a hint of chest hair, she acknowledged, feeling her attraction to him intensify. And how relaxed he seems today. With the wine-grape harvest about to start, Stefano seems to have left early for his labors. No doubt his absence is partly responsible. Of course, Umberto's improvement also must have a lot to do with it.

Emilia was already seated in one of Umberto's high-backed bishop's chairs when they knocked at his door a short time later. Getting to her feet with the stiffness of age, she nodded a greeting as they walked in. Apparently having asserted her right as the sick man's wife to be present, Anna smiled at them from the window seat, where she was stationed with her knitting.

Sunk in the antique four-poster that dominated the room, Umberto had drifted back to sleep. His complexion was gray, and his cheeks were haggard. Arising as if from some massive pipe organ inside him, his snores rocked the room.

Paolo's grip on Laura's hand tightened as he stared at his grandfather. "Mommy?" he whispered.

Emilia didn't fail to catch the apprehension in his voice. Leaning over Umberto, she shook him gently by the shoulders. "Wake up," she urged. "They're here...Guy's wife and his little boy."

Laura drew in a startled breath as the sick man's eyes opened. Like Guy's, they were gold-flecked hazel—twin points of youth and light in the devastation of his face. A rush of guttural speech flowed from him as he held out his good hand in supplication.

"Speak English, Father," Enzo suggested gently. "Laura knows some Italian. But Paolo's just a child. He hasn't had time to learn it yet."

"Of course. Of course. He's American. I forget."

Distorted though they were by the series of strokes that had impaired his speech, Laura discovered that Umberto's remarks were quite intelligible if she paid close attention. As she watched, his ruined face creased in a shaky smile that was swamped by tears.

Slipping into the room, Cristina gave them an antagonistic look. To Laura, her unspoken indictment was clear. *You're going to be the death of him.*

His hand resting lightly at the small of her back, Enzo invited her and Paolo to move a little closer to the bed. "It's all right," he said encouragingly. "You haven't done anything to upset him. This is bound to be an emotional moment for him."

His eyes wide, Paolo cooperated reluctantly. He jumped and gave Laura a panic-stricken look when Umberto tried to touch him.

With a sigh, the sick man let his hand fall back to the coverlet. "How long you stay?" he asked, meeting Laura's eyes.

This was the man who'd sent Guy packing. The one who'd disinherited him, turned him into an exile from both family and country for the terrible sin of following his heart. Malevolent and powerful, he'd vowed Guy wouldn't work again in Italy, even if it meant he had to bribe every oversight committee, buy every racecourse.

In the flesh, ravaged by his illness, he looked pathetic.

She tried to smile. "Longer than I planned . . . nearly two and a half weeks."

"Is not long enough. Your boy. . . he get to know his grandfather, yes? Appreciate his Italian heritage?"

When she'd left Chicago, she'd given Carol her word. She couldn't stay longer, if only for business reasons. In addition, the undercurrents she sensed among the Rossis, particularly those involving Cristina and her obvious fear that Paolo's acceptance would undermine her son's chances of inheriting control of Rossi Motorworks, were uncomfortable to witness.

You don't want to leave Enzo, her inner woman objected. Though he's just your brother-in-law, there's an incredible bond between you. It's as if an invisible silver cord binds you together. She only wished she could believe it was an entirely positive one.

She didn't want Umberto to weep again, either—certainly not on her account. "We'll see," she told him soothingly. "I do agree that Paolo should know you. That's why I agreed to make this trip."

For several seconds, a pin dropping in the room would have shattered the silence like breaking glass.

Then: *"You forgive?"* The once proud auto executive posed the question as if it were laden with years of anguish.

In Laura's opinion, it probably was. "Signor Rossi, *please,*" she protested, unwilling to shed her prejudices so quickly. "I wasn't involved in the situation you're referring to. When you and Guy quarreled . . ."

"You were his wife. Now he is gone, you are . . . *only* one who can forgive me. I was wrong . . . wrong, you understand? . . . to treat him that way!"

A muscle twitched beside Emilia's mouth, as if she were hearing the admission for the first time and regretting that it had been so long in coming. But she didn't intercede. Neither did Enzo. Or Anna. Behind them, Cristina was a silent, angry presence.

Declining to look at Enzo for guidance or let Cristina's wrath sway her, Laura searched her heart. Guy's father was asking for absolution. Though he'd been autocratic, even cruel, how could she withhold mercy?

"I forgive . . . what Guy would surely have forgiven if the two of you could have talked this way," she said at last, coming to terms with the need to be compassionate after years of resentment on her late husband's behalf. "Your son loved you, Signor Rossi. If he were standing here beside me this morning, I'm sure he'd want me to tell you so."

Though tears welled up in Umberto's eyes a second time, they didn't spill over. Reaching out again with his good hand, he squeezed her fingers, lightly ruffled Paolo's blond hair. "We talk, yes, *bambino?*" he asked.

A sensitive child, Paolo clearly realized the equation had changed. This time he didn't flinch. "Okay, Grandpa Rossi," he said, using the unfamiliar name that, during their flight from Milan to Turin, Laura had thought to teach him.

That afternoon, to Paolo's delight, Enzo showed them around the villa property in a pony cart. It was a good deal more extensive than Laura had realized. Though it was Sunday, supposedly a day of rest, on the southern slope of hill after undulating hill, farm workers wearing hats to shade their faces from the sun were pulling dead leaves from the staked vines and repositioning green ones so that they wouldn't crowd the jewellike clusters of ripening fruit. Now and then they would pinch off a few individual grapes and place them in small canvas sacks they carried for the purpose.

Paolo was situated between Laura and Enzo on the pony cart's wooden seat. "Why are they doing that?" he demanded. "Why don't they pick the whole bunch?"

"Because they're not ready to pick yet, nephew." Giving the reins a tug and nickering to the pony, Enzo glanced affectionately at the boy, as if he approved of his interest. "The grapes in the little sacks will go to Stefano, so he can test them for their sugar and acid content,'' he explained. "When they're sweet enough and the acidity's just right, we all get to work in the fields... even your great-grandmother. To make the best wine, grapes have to be picked at the moment of their perfection.''

Brushing aside the odd feeling of déjà vu the Villa Voglia property aroused in her, particularly its five-hundred-year-old stone stable, Laura turned toward him on the seat. "Will we be allowed to help, too?'' she asked.

Enzo grinned. "Of course. You're family. It's expected.''

I don't feel like family where Cristina and Emilia are concerned, she answered silently. But with you... Anna... and perhaps Umberto one day, if he lives long enough...

Seconds later, their eyes met, and it was as if they were thinking a single thought—one with life-shaping repercussions for them both. We may be family, but it's more than that, Laura reflected as they drove along a dirt track between vine-planted rows in the September sunlight. We've known each other forever. I know it sounds crazy. That's just how it is.

She wasn't sure she trusted Enzo to be the other she'd discovered in him. Or even that she *wanted* him to be. She had the uncomfortable feeling that getting too close to him would draw her even deeper into the mystery posed by her dizzy spells and the haunting sense of familiarity the Villa Voglia evoked. Somehow, the phenomena seemed linked.

Turning the pony into a wider lane that led to the winery, and giving him a minimum of guidance, Enzo continued to gaze at her over the top of Paolo's blond head. Having him look at her that way was like falling into the fund of things. She felt invigorated, out of control, utterly powerless to stop what was happening.

"I have to return to the factory for a few days, beginning tomorrow, to catch up on a backlog of work," he said apologetically as their extraordinary wordless communication continued unabated. "I'll be back to help with the harvest...by Thursday at the latest. If you need me for anything in the meantime, you have only to call."

The statement was prosaic in the extreme. Yet, like that of his lingering handshake when they'd said good-night at her front door the day they met, its promise went deeper than a kiss. Henceforth, we'll be connected...like it or not, she thought with a little shiver of anticipation. Or maybe I should say *re*connected.

Chapter Five

For Laura, the days Enzo spent in Turin were like a quilt patched together of indolence, uncertainty and expectation. Little by little, she settled into a role she'd never expected to play—that of Rossi daughter-in-law. Cosseted by servants and accepted by the family's most powerful members, she was free to roam the magnificent country house and estate where her late husband had spent his childhood. Yet she didn't let herself relax unduly. Something whispered that, if she let down her guard too much, she'd fall prey to a danger she couldn't articulate.

Every morning after breakfast, she and Paolo paid Umberto a visit in his room. Remaining in the background as much as possible during those sessions, she encouraged her son to talk to his grandfather and ask him questions. The old man responded with stories and awkward bursts of affection. Though he continued to shrink from the latter, gradually the boy's comfort level grew.

From her vantage point as onlooker and arbitrator, Umberto's emotions weren't difficult to estimate. He clearly loved her child and saw him as a claim to immortality—maybe even a replacement for the son he'd driven from his doorstep. Whatever the case, their visits appeared to be therapeutic for him. By Wednesday morning, the ailing auto magnate had recovered sufficiently to spend an hour chatting with them on the balcony outside his room.

Each afternoon, during Paolo's nap, Laura wandered the villa grounds, sketching scenes she hoped to render more completely in pastel when she returned to Chicago. As she did, she found herself repeatedly choosing the stable as a subject, and turning to the pencil drawing she'd made in Chicago based on the Renaissance nobleman's portrait. He belongs here, at the Villa Voglia...as do I, she thought, without any basis in fact to support the notion. Since her arrival in Italy, it seemed, her life in Chicago had shrunk in importance, until she felt as if she'd lived it in another dimension, as another person.

With the annual wine-grape harvest about to get under way, she barely saw Stefano. Laboring from dawn to dusk, he didn't appear at the dinner table. Once Enzo had departed, neither did Cristina or Sofia. Murmuring something about business-related social obligations, the former had returned with 'Nardo to Turin to spend a few days with her husband before returning to help with the harvest. Blithely self-absorbed, the latter had departed for the Riviera with only the briefest of farewells to her father.

Neutral where Sofia was concerned, Laura didn't mourn Cristina's absence, or that of Stefano. From the first, the younger Rossi daughter had made no secret of the fact that she deplored their presence at the Villa Voglia. As for the half brother turned estate manager, though she felt a modicum of sympathy for him, his calculating, almost prurient gaze made her decidedly uncomfortable.

During the span of those languid, luminous autumn days, she got to know Anna a little better. Together they joined Margherita in the kitchen to make *agnolotti*—an activity she suspected Anna's own daughters would have spurned—and drove to visit a museum in Alba that contained Roman and prehistoric antiquities. To her surprise, Emilia, too, made an effort to cultivate her. Inviting her for coffee in her private sitting room, the Rossi matriarch quietly pressed her to extend her visit.

As his return from Turin neared, Enzo and the extraordinary soul-deep harmony that had flowed between them during their Sunday tour of the estate were never far from her thoughts. Neither were the dark side she sensed in him—one that seemed oddly foreign to the man she'd met in Chicago—and the link she perceived between him and the sense of déjà vu that plagued her.

Daydreaming about him Wednesday afternoon as she wandered into the villa's kitchen garden with basket and shears to gather flowers for a centerpiece, she didn't realize, at first, that one of her "attacks" was imminent. Seconds later, her posture sagged. The garden's herbs and blossoms and lettuces appeared to dissolve into a thousand shining fragments.

As they had during her second spell at the Art Institute, the inhabitants of another era who seemed to people the air close to where she stood remained mostly peripheral. She felt rather than saw the man in a velvet doublet who whispered urgently in her ear, "Marry me, Rafaella."

The voice seemed almost to be Enzo's. And yet it wasn't. It was her name though she'd have sworn on a stack of bibles she'd never heard it before. It sank irretrievably from consciousness when Anna touched her arm.

"Are you all right?" her mother-in-law asked with a worried frown. "I happened to come out on the terrace. When I saw you slump like that, with the shears trailing from your hand, I was afraid you might fall and hurt yourself.''

"I'm fine. *Really*." Struggling to piece together her composure, Laura turned to Anna with what she hoped was a convincing smile. "It was probably the heat," she said. "And an empty stomach. When Emilia mentioned that the picking is to start tomorrow, I got too excited to eat very much. Neither Paolo nor I have had a chance to participate in anything like that...."

The barrage of words had the desired effect. Though Anna didn't appear completely convinced, she didn't ask any further questions.

Enzo arrived at twilight, his white Falconetta convertible churning up the drive in a cloud of dust. Seated on the balustrade of the Villa Voglia's front terrace, where she'd gone to think about what had happened in the garden that afternoon, Laura got to her feet. The long, fluid skirt of her silk crepe dress, which was printed with morning glories in shades of blue and violet, fluttered about her ankles. Part of her wanted to slip into the house so that she wouldn't have to face him. The other part yearned to fling itself into his arms.

If avoiding him had genuinely been her aim, it was already too late. Getting out of the car and taking the steps to the terrace with easy grace, Enzo laced his fingers through hers so that the vulnerable little interstices between them were touching. Effortlessly, for good or ill, the bond she'd felt in the pony cart reestablished itself.

"How are things?" he asked her in a low voice.

Her sense that they were strongly linked wasn't dispelled by his casual choice of words. Filled with speculation and a curious kind of knowing, it seemed to expand until it was limitless. In her fantasy life, she realized, he'd become both sweetheart and protector. Why, then, did a still, small voice inside her confide that to love him would be to risk? *He's connected to the portrait, and to your dizzy spells,* it whispered. *If you get involved with him, you'll be sucked even deeper into the past scenarios that haunt you.*

"Things are fine," she answered, refusing to listen.

The mere fact of his hands clasping hers was exquisitely suggestive. Responding to it, her nipples tightened. God help her, but she wanted him to touch them—stroke them through the whisper-weight fabric of her bodice and coax them into even greater prominence.

"Your father's better," she added, consumed with a need to say something, anything, that would defuse the situation. "He and Paolo have been getting along very well. I've been getting to know the lay of the land and working on some sketches . . . not doing very much, I'm afraid."

Gazing down at her and feeling himself quicken in response to the allure of her softly parted lips, Enzo yearned to tug her against his body. Too well he could imagine how her breasts would feel, pressing against his chest. It was a long time since he'd made love to anyone.

I'm not the powder keg unfit for feminine companionship Stefano would have me believe, he thought. I have as much right as any man to reach out for what I need and want. Yet he had a poor record of controlling his temper, at least where Stefano was concerned. The argument with his former fiancée that had resulted in a near-fatal accident was a case in point. He didn't want Laura to suffer similarly at his hands.

Speaking to fill the silence, he willed his longing to subside. "Tomorrow we pick the grapes."

Though Laura couldn't follow his train of thought, she'd watched the play of emotion on his face. She'd felt the pull of his desire, and she'd felt him withdraw from her, at least figuratively.

"I know," she answered. "Emilia announced it at lunch. Maybe it sounds childish to an old hand like yourself, but I'm thrilled at the chance to be part of it."

"I don't consider it childish. I feel the same excitement every year, and I've done it for as long as I can remember." Allowing himself to drape one arm lightly about her shoulders, he drew her into the loggia. "Come," he urged, his voice pleasantly rough in the privacy of that shadowed, partly enclosed space. "Look in on Father with me. And keep me company while I eat a bite of supper."

Nothing has actually happened to hint that we're more than in-laws, or acquaintances ripening into friends, she thought as they said good-night an hour or so later in the second-floor hallway outside her room. Yet the flame of my involvement with him keeps burning brighter.

"No lying awake, thinking about tomorrow," he said, his face relaxing into a smile as the light touch of his hand seared her waist through her dress's pliant fabric. "We start before dawn, you know, with breakfast under the trees. Plus, it's a hard day's physical labor."

Though a cavalcade of dreams wound their way through Laura's sleep as night ebbed toward morning, she couldn't remember any of them when Gemma knocked and entered to tell her it was time to dress. Outside, the sky was the color of pitch, as deep as velvet. The tall French doors that led from her room to an adjoining balcony had been thrown open to admit the air, and through them she could hear car doors slamming, people laughing and calling to each other. Cristina's voice, as she gave 'Nardo his marching orders, reached her from the hallway.

"I'm ready, *signora*. I can dress the little one for you, if you like, before I go down to wait on the table," the maid offered as Laura stretched and threw back the covers.

Her mind full of Enzo and the prospect of working at his side in the earthy process of picking the grapes, she gratefully accepted. Washing her face and brushing her teeth, she pulled on a pair of faded jeans, along with a blouse, a sweatshirt, an indigo-and-white bandanna and a pair of slightly oversize boots Gemma had provided. It occurred to her that the grass and the bare, crumbly soil between the rows of vines would be wet with dew. Until the sun came up, she suspected, it would be damp and cool.

By the time she approached the long communal table and the collection of mismatched, dilapidated folding chairs that had been set up beneath several broadly arching plane trees near the villa's rear terrace, dawn had begun to finger-paint the sky.

Thanks to the villa's powerful exterior lights and the tall kerosene torches on poles Stefano had caused to be stuck in the earth to augment them, she could see everyone's faces quite clearly. With the exception of Umberto, who'd remained upstairs with Gemma's sister from Alba to keep an eye on him, every member of the Rossi family and their staff was present. In addition, workers and landowners from neighboring farms and estates, the friendly local postman—even the Rossis' parish priest—had arrived to help.

The mouth-watering aroma of eggs baked with cheese, huge platters of ham and sausages and steaming bowls of polenta filled the air. To Laura's surprise, red table wine was served, in addition to coffee and fruit juice. Apparently the harvest is a Dionysian business in more ways than one, she thought.

Enzo appeared and scooped a still-sleepy Paolo up in his arms. "Come...sit with me, you two," he invited, the buoyant side of his personality clearly uppermost at that moment. "We'll ride out together after we eat, so I can give you the proper instruction."

As the workers-to-be wolfed down gargantuan portions, the talk was mostly about the vintage and the degree of sugar in the grapes, though many stories and jokes linked with past harvests were traded across the table. At last, Margherita's magnificent repast had been reduced to a pile of scraps and dirty dishes. The sun was up. Several rented flatbed trucks, as well as the Rossi farm cart, pulled by old Michele, the gardener, with his tractor, stood ready to convey the pickers to the fields.

Lifting Paolo into the back of one of the trucks, Enzo climbed aboard and gave Laura a hand up. In the truck bed, her little boy snuggled in her lap, his drowsiness returning with the early hour and a full stomach. As they bumped along the dirt track where, a few days earlier, she'd looked into Enzo's eyes and discovered a bond that seemed to surpass by centuries their limited knowledge of each other, Laura drew up her knees to make additional room for a young farmer and his wife. With a keen awareness of whose it was, she allowed her neck to rest against the strong right arm positioned around her shoulders.

At their drop-off point, a hill distant enough from the villa that its roof and dovecote were barely visible above the trees, they strapped special picking baskets to their backs. The baskets' shape would allow them to bend over and dump the grapes into big plastic bins with a minimum of effort, Enzo explained.

Paolo and the handful of other children who'd accompanied them received smaller baskets, with handles. Unlike the adults, who would cut whole bunches of fruit free from the vines with small, sharp knives, the children would break off more modest clusters with their fingers.

"They pick for the chance to learn and for the sense of accomplishment it provides . . . not to increase the profit or our efficiency," Enzo told her.

As she'd expected, the ground between the rows of vines was still soaked with dew. Droplets of moisture clung to each leaf like jewels, scattering at the touch, and ornamenting the grapes' dusky sheen. Beginning to work her way down a row, with Enzo laboring a few feet away, she drank the fruit's rich, winey scent into her nostrils. I'm not sure which is the headier...their aroma or his nearness, she thought. Her inner woman, she knew, had already dispensed with such questions.

By 10:00 a.m., it was warm enough that Laura could remove her sweatshirt and knot it by the sleeves around her waist. Exuberant as young colts, Paolo and the other children were doing more playing than picking.

"This is actual work," she commented to Enzo, straightening and wiping her forehead.

"Ah, but *what* work!" He flashed her a brilliant smile, for the first time since she'd known him clearly content to his bones' marrow. "To use one's hands instead of one's head," he added, "and be a cog in the process that produces wine for our table, rather than overseeing it...for me, that's extraordinarily satisfying."

She was ravenous when, around noon, the trucks that had lumbered down to the winery with the most recent load of grapes returned with wine, soda, fruit and huge piles of sandwiches made with freshly baked semolina loaves and filled with prosciutto, salami and mortadella, along with pepperoncini, assorted cheeses and slices of fresh tomato. From their stations on separate trucks, Margherita and Gemma sliced off portions of the filled loaves with carving knives.

The pickers ate on a mismatched collection of old quilts and blankets in the grassy areas that verged on the tracks between the vines. Seated with Anna and the parish priest in the only folding chairs provided, Emilia persuaded Paolo to spread his jacket on the ground beside her and join them for the meal. Before long, though, he'd eaten his fill and slipped away to run and shout with the other children.

Laura and Enzo had the remains of a ragged, once pretty quilt to themselves. As they ate and quaffed wine from paper cups, their knees were almost touching. Gesturing as he spoke, Enzo explained that roughly two-thirds of the year's crop had been purchased by a large commercial winemaker, leaving the balance to be crushed and fermented for an estate bottling.

Now and then their fingers brushed, causing a tingle of excitement to pass between them. They were sitting so close that Laura could smell the faint tang of his perspiration blending with the aroma of sun-warmed skin and the citrus-based after-shave she associated with his expensive designer suits. *At some point, the barriers have come down between us,* she acknowledged as she gazed into the expressive brown eyes that reminded her of her Renaissance nobleman. *Enzo's not a stranger. I don't think of him as my brother-in-law, but as a man I could far too easily love.*

As she did when it came to letting her guard down with the Rossi family and allowing herself the full range of her emotions where the villa was concerned, she shrank from fully investing herself in a relationship with him. It only made sense to do so, she tried to tell herself. Their time together would necessarily be brief. Once she returned to America, they'd see very little of each other.

Yet she knew there was another, more compelling reason for her hesitation. Relaxed and affable though he seemed most of the time, she sensed Enzo had a darker side. Instinct argued it could be a trap for her.

At last it was time for them to head back into the rows if they were to complete the harvest while the grapes were at their peak. Scrambling to his feet, Enzo offered her a hand up. Their fingers were briefly laced as Stefano arrived and paused for a sandwich. *So... that's how it is between the two of you*, his level look told them. Self-conscious beneath the electron microscope of his gaze, Laura caught Emilia watching them with much the same expression.

Thanks to the morning's work, they'd established an efficient work rhythm, and the afternoon picking went well. By six o'clock or thereabouts, the vines were largely stripped of their fruit. Grubby, tired, their muscles pleasantly loose from physical labor, they rode back toward the villa on the farm cart, pulled by Michele's tractor. At a word from Enzo, the old gardener dropped them off at the winery. Predictably, it was a hive of activity, with workmen from the estate loading the grapes destined for the commercial winemaker into several large trucks.

"What about the Rossi vintage?" Laura asked.

Enzo set Paolo on his feet. "Come see," he said, motioning them toward the old stone building's cavernous entrance. "They're already being separated."

If she thought she'd inhaled a strong, fruity aroma in the fields, Laura realized, she hadn't experienced anything yet. Inside the ancient winery, which Enzo said had been built around 1720, some two hundred years after the stables that had so captured her interest, several of the Rossis' year-round laborers were operating a small thresher. It mechanically separated the stems from the fruit. From it, the grapes were sucked up a clear plastic tube and ejected into a large stainless steel vat, where they would undergo their first fermenting.

"The juice from the fruit itself is almost clear," Enzo related. "So we leave the skins on for the crushing. That's where all the color is. A few of the stems will get through, and that's all right. The tannin in them helps the wine age, and gives it a faintly herbaceous quality."

He went on to explain that a cloth would be placed over the vat to keep out fruit flies. In the morning, yeast would be added. The "Brix," the sugar content of the mix, would be scientifically corrected.

"To give the devil his due," he said, unconsciously voicing his ingrained dislike of his half brother, "Stefano knows the process to perfection."

Having missed his nap and spent an entire day outdoors, Paolo was cross, not to mention incredibly dirty, by the time they reached the house. His face streaked with earth and grape juice from the vineyard, he clung to Laura, whining and complaining like an irritable two-year-old.

"I'd better give him a bath before supper, if he's to have one at all," she decided. "Once he's eaten, his head will be ready to hit the pillow."

Affectionately Enzo ruffled the boy's hair. "See you at the table, then. Like this morning, we'll be eating outdoors, as a group. Perhaps I ought to warn you...it's not polite to shower, though it's all right to wash your hands and face. Our volunteers have to line up outside at the pump, and we don't like to exercise an advantage over them."

Parting company with him, she and Paolo went inside. As they started upstairs toward their shared bathroom on the villa's second floor, a balding, bespectacled man in a business suit with a briefcase under his arm emerged from Umberto's room. He glanced at Paolo with obvious interest and wished them good-afternoon as he passed them, going in the opposite direction.

To Laura, the man was a complete stranger. Immediately she thought of Umberto's condition. Had Gemma's sister been forced to summon a doctor?

"Is anything wrong?" she demanded as the maid's curly-headed sibling appeared and followed the stranger downstairs, carrying a tray laden with empty coffee cups.

Though the girl's answer was negative, Laura's worries didn't evaporate. "Who was that man?" she persisted. *"Dottore?"*

Gemma's sister shook her head, clearly anxious to cut off the flow of questions. "A business acquaintance of Signor Rossi's, I believe, *signora,*" she replied in nervous Italian, almost as if she'd been coached not to elaborate.

Laura forgot the incident as she washed her face and supervised Paolo's splashing in their joint bathtub, which had whale-shaped brass handles and old-fashioned claw feet. After a day of sun and grime, a warm, wet washcloth followed by a light film of moisturizer felt heavenly on her face. Enzo told me not to shower, but he didn't say anything about brushing the tangles from my hair or putting on a fresh dab of lipstick, she thought. Using the mirror over the antique pedestal sink as her guide, she indulged herself by doing both.

The day's color had bled from the sky and someone had relit the torches by the time she and Paolo rejoined their fellow harvesters at the table. As before, wine flowed freely. There were a number of elaborate, sentimental toasts.

His hands already gnarled from manual labor, though he was just twenty-five or so, the young farmer who'd ridden out to the vineyards with them that morning was strumming a guitar. An older man with a drooping mustache joined him on an accordion as Enzo pulled out chairs for himself, Laura and Paolo. Simultaneously, Margherita and Gemma arrived with huge platters of food. Knives clattered. Pasta was wound expertly around forks. The din of talk and laughter escalated.

Though by then their stomachs would be full and their tired muscles beginning to ache, Enzo had said, the hours after dinner were reserved for dancing and storytelling. "With the wine and music to prop us up, we don't feel the painful effects of our work until morning," he'd told her.

Slipping out of her chair near the end of the meal, Laura took Paolo inside and put him to bed. For once he didn't beg for a story or insist she remain until he fell asleep. Instead, he turned his back on her without a word and snuggled deeper beneath the covers.

It was fully dark by the time she reemerged from the house. In the interim, a light breeze had come up, causing the flames of the torches to shudder and dance. Already quite a few couples, including some old enough to be grandparents many times over, were dancing. Enzo's chair at the table was empty. Hanging back at the edge of the crowd, Laura tried to spot him, but couldn't. *No doubt he's dancing with that skinny twenty-year-old who kept eyeing us this afternoon,* she speculated. *But then, why shouldn't he? He's the official host of the harvest now that his father's bedridden.*

She'd just have to face it. There had been women in Enzo's life before they met, and there would be others after she returned to America. For all she knew, he'd spent his nights away in Turin in a lover's bed. He was too vital, too sexual, a man to be celibate. She'd do well to drop her romantic notions.

The likelihood that he's involved in one or more affairs is just part of the problem, her inner self whispered, tugging her in a direction she was even less willing to go. *For all his warmth and seeming nonchalance, he's deeply troubled about something. Learning to care for him would mean letting go of every handhold.*

On the verge of seeking out Anna and offering to sit with her to watch the dancers, Laura almost jumped when Enzo slipped an arm around her waist. "So... there you are," he murmured beside her ear. "I was about to send out a search party. I've been looking forward to dancing with you."

Helpless to go against her feelings for him, despite her nagging sense that they could mean trouble to each other, she let him pull her close. Simultaneously, the guitarist and the accordion player took up a catchy, wistful ballad. It was vaguely familiar, and after a moment Laura managed to

place it. Stefano had performed it on his harmonica the
night of her arrival. Already the gathering on the terrace
that had occasioned his performance seemed part of the
distant past. She felt as if she had known the Villa Voglia for
centuries, had sought shelter in Enzo's embrace for as long
as she could remember.

On a downbeat, they began to move. Though she was
wearing jeans, not a party dress, and close-cut, thoroughly
trampled grass cushioned their feet instead of polished par-
quet, threading the crush of dirty, slightly inebriated grape-
pickers with Enzo was luxury beyond measure.

How can I be expected to think of caution, consider
practicality, she demanded, when I can feel his heart
beat . . . his thighs brush mine as if he lusts for them to cra-
dle him? Almost from the moment they'd met, the neglected voluptuary in her had longed to know what it would
be like to move in tandem with him. Now she had her wish.
She considered it right as rain, or heaven.

Washed by little waves of feeling as he tugged her closer,
the warm, deep glow between her legs intensified. Shud-
ders of anticipation spread over her skin from every point
of contact. In bed, she raged, we'd flow together like lava,
like light, burning and fusing in a symphony of rapture and
exploration.

His self-control plummeting to its nadir, Enzo was
thinking similar thoughts. This is what I imagined as I
tossed and turned in my bed at the Palazzo Rossi, he admitted to himself. The world receding, and Laura mine to
hold. In his mind's eye, he pictured them rolling naked in
the huge four-poster where, for too long, he'd been the sole
occupant.

He felt rather than heard her gasp of pleasure as the evidence of his need pressed more blatantly against her. It was
as incendiary, as inflammatory, as setting a match to dry
grass. We can't take each other in the house, he reasoned

wildly, the wine he'd drunk singing in his blood. But there's always the stable. Together, on the hay...

Like heat lightning briefly illuminating the night sky without heralding a drop of rain, a wisp of the recurring nightmare that troubled him cut across his imaginings and then was gone. A moment later, the music faltered. Someone had poured fresh libations for the musicians, and they'd decided to take a break. Laughing and talking with their arms entwined, the other dancers strolled back to the table.

Enzo didn't follow suit. Instead, he drew Laura more deeply into the shadows. Her heart in her throat, she didn't protest. Screened from curious eyes by a minivan that was parked beyond the nearest circle of torchlight, she let him enfold her. A sigh escaped her as his mouth covered hers.

Chapter Six

Released from the bonds of separateness the brevity of their acquaintance had imposed on them, Laura pressed her body against Enzo's as he invaded her mouth. Yes, she thought fiercely. *Yes.* I want to give you everything. Finding her way in the erotic wilderness of his kiss, she caressed his shoulders through the barrier of his sweat-stained shirt as she reciprocated. How sweet, how strong, his arms were. How sheltering. Flagrant instruments of desire, their tongues dueled in a heated imitation of the loving congress they both wanted so much.

With a little explosion of need, Enzo grasped her by the seat of her jeans and positioned her more tellingly against his arousal. I don't want to saddle you with the curse of my temper, or the black, moody periods that erupt into nightmarish dreams, he pleaded silently. Yet how am I to live if we can't have each other?

Every fiber of his being, and every ounce of energy he possessed, pleaded with him to make love to her—to fuse their longings in one delirious amalgam of exploration. With every breath, every whimper of pleasure, she was telling him she wanted the same thing. A desire for completion so strong he had never known its equal had him thinking of places where they could be alone. Stiffening at the crunch of shoe leather against a fragment of glass or metal that someone had left lying in the grass, they moved apart. The abrasive sound of a match striking was accompanied by a whiff of sulfur. Abruptly their cloak of shadows was torn away by a little *whoosh* of flame.

"Oh, it's you," Stefano said tonelessly. "Sorry. I thought someone was breaking into the parish van."

Staring at him in the split second it took him to blow out the match and turn on his heel, Laura felt like a deer caught in a hunter's sights. He *knew* it was us, she thought. He's been watching us all evening. Though she had no objective reason for thinking so, she was convinced Stefano would run straight to Emilia with a report.

Enzo's face was contorted with anger. "Damn him!" he exclaimed, shoving fist to palm, his voice so bitter she barely recognized it. "There's no end to his provocations!"

Her passionate surge of conviction that they belonged together draining away, Laura found herself once more hobbled by uncertainty. Since they'd met two weeks earlier, a deeply primitive part of her had shunned involvement, even though she was powerfully drawn to him.

"What happened was my fault as much as yours," she said. "Let's just forget it, okay? I'm awfully tired, thanks to our work in the vineyard today. If you don't mind, instead of returning to the party, I think I'll go to bed."

We might have spent the night together if Stefano hadn't interfered, Enzo countered silently, struggling to regain control. It galled him more than he cared to admit that, in a way, his half brother had done him a favor. Laura was his sister-in-law. Guy's widow. He couldn't lure her to the sta-

ble for an hour's extemporaneous passion. Or carry her off
to Turin without making family-sanctioned arrangements.
She had her reputation and her son to think about.

A brief affair wasn't in the cards for them. Before he
could let himself reach for more, they'd have to talk.
Though the truth might put her off, he owed it to her to tell
her about his recurring nightmares—and the circumstances
under which his engagement to Luciana Paraggi had ended.
There was also the problem of their living and earning their
daily bread half a world away from each other. A week of
her proposed two-and-a-half-week stay in Italy had elapsed
already.

Hell . . . maybe the best thing for all concerned would be
for him to keep his distance. "At least let me walk you to the
house," he urged in a low growl, unwilling for the moment
to relinquish contact with her.

If she agreed, Laura knew, he'd kiss her again. And
they'd both be lost. "I'd rather you didn't, Enzo," she
whispered. "After what took place a few minutes ago, I
need time to think. I'll see you at breakfast."

Despite Laura's weariness, falling asleep that night was a
lengthy process. Her brain couldn't seem to stop going over
what had happened, from the splendor of Enzo's kiss to
Stefano's intrusion and their subsequent awkwardness. In
fact, it seemed bent on reviewing every word and gesture
that had passed between them. As she buried her face
against her pillow, wantonly imagining it to be Enzo's
shoulder, she couldn't help but think of what would have
transpired if Stefano hadn't interrupted them.

Emotionally as well as physically exhausted, she sank at
last into a relatively dreamless slumber. She didn't stir at
first when, shortly after sunrise, harsh words erupted in the
hallway outside her room. Gradually the voices grew louder
and more contentious. Blinking the sleep from her eyes, she
realized Enzo and Cristina were arguing.

"You're responsible for this!" Cristina was saying accusingly in rapid-fire Italian. "You brought them here. Father didn't *ask* you to. Now they've wormed themselves into his good graces. And 'Nardo will be the one to suffer for it!"

Enzo's response was lower, huskier, than his sister's, a bit more difficult to catch. Straining her ears and her knowledge of the language they were speaking, Laura thought she heard him reply that, while Umberto hadn't previously confessed his desire to mend the family rift, he'd voiced his gratitude for their coming many times since.

"They're family...every bit as much as Vittorio and 'Nardo are," Enzo added forcefully, his voice rising in volume again. "Paolo's his grandson, too...as worthy as your brat of a son to inherit. Maybe it's time you got used to it."

Had Umberto changed his will to include Paolo? Laura didn't have time to speculate—not if she wanted to catch Cristina's caustic retort.

"I'll *never* get used to it!" her sister-in-law vowed emphatically. "Or accept the fact that you coerced him into legitimizing that fortune hunter's child because you want to go to bed with her!"

Biting back a cry of protest, Laura could feel the blood rushing to her cheeks. Meanwhile, Enzo's fury knew no bounds. "Slander me if you like," he threatened. "But I'd watch what I said about Laura, if I were you. I don't care if you *are* my sister."

Cristina remained defiant. "And if I don't choose to comply?" she retorted. "What will you do about it?"

He didn't answer, at least not in words. In her canopied bed, separated from the warring siblings by an expanse of priceless Venetian carpet and the visual barrier of a gilded and paneled wooden door, Laura imagined him catching his sister by the wrist and digging his fingers into her flesh. Though the undercurrent of moodiness and anger she'd sensed in him made her uneasy, to say the least, she couldn't fault him. She herself would gladly have wrung Cristina's lovely neck.

"Father's an old man. Sick. His mind's been affected," Cristina went on in a ringing tone. "When he dies, I guarantee it . . . Vittorio and I will contest!"

Again Enzo didn't challenge her out loud. The ensuing silence was deafening, broken after several seconds by the sound of Enzo's footsteps descending the stairs and Cristina's heels clicking on the marble tiles of the upstairs hall as she retreated toward her father's room.

Hugging her knees beneath her embroidered coverlet, Laura felt sick to her stomach. The worst has happened, she thought. My tryst with Enzo has become common knowledge. The family is quarreling over us.

The phenomenon of the stranger emerging from Umberto's room with a briefcase under his arm during the harvest had been explained with a vengeance. Choosing a time when he knew everyone would be occupied—in order to sidestep confrontation, apparently—the ailing auto magnate had made her son one of his heirs.

Though I'll defend Paolo's rights as a Rossi to the death, just as I'd have defended Guy's, I never hoped for anything like this, she thought. Never wanted it. Thanks to the settlement that had resulted from Guy's accident, in addition to Guy's inheritance from his maternal grandmother and the living she earned for them, her little boy would never lack for anything.

Whether or not Cristina fought her father's decision, she didn't plan to intervene. That being the case, she decided, maybe she ought to pack. And see about changing their tickets. With luck, we could return home today, she thought, warming to her hastily conceived plan as she threw back the bed covers.

Leaving for America at once would have the added benefit of putting a stop to her budding relationship with Enzo. I'll have to consult him about transportation to the airport in Turin, she thought. And I know what his reaction will be. He'll beg me to remain, for his father's sake. I'll have to be firm with him . . . admit I overheard his quarrel with his sister, if need be, to gain his cooperation.

For several days, Gemma had been getting Paolo up each morning, seeing to it that he brushed his teeth and helping him lace up his tennis shoes—a task she'd assumed out of growing fondness for him, Laura guessed. That morning she considered the maid's help a particular boon. If she hurried, she'd have time to make the necessary arrangements without raising too many questions on Paolo's part. He'd probably accept their early return as a given if it was presented to him that way.

Descending the stairs a few minutes later in striped T-shirt, slacks and espadrilles, she heard a car take off as if the devil were in hot pursuit. Enzo? she wondered. Had he left for Turin without saying goodbye—or giving her and Paolo a chance to hitch a ride to the airport? Crossing the *sala* at a dead run and racing through the loggia, she reached the villa's front terrace in time to see Cristina's champagne-beige Rossi sedan disappear around a bend in the drive.

Thank heaven I needn't deal with *her* this morning, she thought. Braving Enzo and Emilia at breakfast will be enough. She only prayed that, before taking off in a cloud of dust and outrage, Cristina hadn't upset her father too much.

The breakfast nook having been given over to food preparation the day before because of the overflow from the villa kitchen, that morning's repast was served in the dining room. Though Laura quickly surmised that Stefano had left early for the winery in order to supervise the addition of the yeast to the mash, Enzo, Anna and Emilia were at the table. Seemingly more tired and fragile than usual, though her posture was ramrod-straight, the Rossi matriarch had dark circles under her eyes, as if she'd gotten little sleep.

Glancing up at Laura's entrance, Enzo read determination in her gaze. She hasn't forgiven me for last night, he thought, aching at the delicate shape of her mouth and remembering how it had felt to kiss it. This morning she'll want me to keep my distance.

Getting to his feet, he pulled out her chair. She took a seat, responding deferentially to the two older women's murmured *"Buon giorno."* An awkward silence ensued as Margherita poured her coffee and Anna passed a plate of crisp, anise-flavored toast.

I'll have to snatch a moment alone with him, Laura thought. I don't want to bring up the subject of an early departure in front of Anna and Emilia before gaining his assistance.

She was forced to revise her strategy a few minutes later, when Enzo touched a napkin to his mouth and remarked that, though it was a Saturday, he'd be returning to his Turin office. From the sound of things, he planned to leave at once.

"What's so important that it can't wait?" Emilia asked, replacing her fragile Haviland coffee cup in its saucer with one blue-veined hand.

In response, Enzo glanced fleetingly at Laura. Considering the personal problems he didn't want to foist on her, he'd give her all the room she wanted. He only hoped she hadn't heard him and Cristina arguing.

"The new union contract," he said. "I planned to go over the final draft yesterday, in time for Monday's meeting. Thanks to the harvest, I wasn't able to."

From Laura's point of view, the story was sheer fabrication. Nothing had prevented Enzo from bringing the contract down to the country with him if he wished to study it at his leisure. He wants to sidestep the controversy over Umberto's will, she thought. And he's had second thoughts of his own about what happened last night. Well, avoiding future temptation shouldn't be too difficult!

"Sorry to bring this up at the breakfast table, but you leave me little choice," she said, feeling very brash and American as she turned to him. "Through no fault of my own, I overheard your conversation with Cristina this morning. In view of what it revealed, and the attitude of, um...certain family members toward us, I think it best Paolo and I return to the States as soon as possible. If you could wait a half hour or so while I pack, I'll be happy to postpone calling the airlines until I can do so from a Turin hotel."

She felt rather than heard his smothered exclamation of distress, and Anna's sharp intake of breath.

Emilia might not reprimand her for being so brusque, but it was too much to hope that she wouldn't exert her authority in the situation. "The last thing we want is for you and Paolo to curtail your visit with us, granddaughter," she said forcefully, addressing Laura in that manner for the first time since her arrival at the Villa Voglia. "That being the case, I'd appreciate it if you'd be frank with us. Are you referring to the change my son made in his will yesterday? And Cristina's unfortunate reaction to it?"

The flush that heated Laura's cheeks was answer enough. Enzo longed to leap to his feet and apologize on his sister's behalf—to reassure Laura that she was free to continue her visit on whatever terms she wished. He'd absent himself for the remainder of her stay, if that would make things easier for her. Out of deference to his grandmother, however, he didn't move or speak.

"I want you and everyone else in this family to know that I approve of what Umberto did yesterday," the Rossi matriarch continued in no uncertain terms. "In fact, I suggested it. A great wrong was perpetrated when Umberto disowned Guy, and now it has been put to rights. If you leave as a result of what he's done, taking Paolo with you, my son's health may not stand the strain."

His face a study in conflicting emotions, Enzo nodded his agreement. Though she didn't speak, Anna seemed to concur by leaning forward in her chair.

For her part, Laura felt a like butterfly pinned to an album page—effectively immobilized. If Umberto had another stroke as a result of their early departure, and it proved fatal, she would be to blame. She'd never forgive herself. Yet, as the target of Cristina's hatred and Enzo's passionate ambivalence, she would find it difficult to remain at the villa....

Seemingly able to read even the ellipses between their thoughts, Emilia appeared to accept a victory as her due. She patted Laura's hand in an uncharacteristic gesture. "Leave Cristina and her husband to me," she advised. "I guarantee they won't insult you further."

On the verge of blurting out a half hearted "Thank-you," Laura stopped herself. But it was plain, even to her, that she'd acquiesced. "All right, then," she said reluctantly, making it official.

The older woman's thin lips curved. "It seems you needn't wait for Laura and Paolo to accompany you after all," she informed Enzo. "Shall we expect you next weekend? Or..."

Though he seemed relieved that she was staying, Laura could tell Enzo wasn't happy with the morning's turn of events. Stubbornly she averted her eyes as he pushed back his chair.

I should have stayed in America for a few weeks...courted her...made love to her there, he was thinking. There's every reason to suppose it would have been glorious. With an ocean separating me from the Villa Voglia, I don't dream of blood on my hands. Or wake up drenched in sweat, re-membering how Luciana's car veered off the Asti road dur-ing our quarrel...

"I'm not sure yet," he temporized, letting his gaze flicker over the delicate, lightly tanned oval of Laura's face, the thick, dark lashes she'd lowered slightly to keep him from reading her thoughts. "If there are problems with the con-tract, we'll have to negotiate. And you know how that goes. It could drag on a bit. Plus, the new Falconetta design has been giving us headaches...."

Not counting the date of their departure, their visit had eight days left to run. I doubt if I'll see him again before he comes to collect us and take us to the airport, Laura thought. If only we could talk without getting tangled up in lust for each other. I'd tell him about my fears, the dizzy spells that have plagued me. Then again, maybe she wouldn't. He might think she was psychoanalysis material, an emotional basket case.

With a flurry of youthful energy, Paolo appeared at the table, volubly demanding her attention. Meanwhile, Emilia had finished her meal. "Come, Enzo," she invited, her wish, as usual, taking the form of a subtle command. "Talk to me in my sitting room before you go. There's something I want to discuss with you."

Enzo didn't return to the dining room or offer Laura any tender goodbyes before getting in his white convertible and roaring off in the direction of the Turin highway. Though in his absence the Rossi country estate was as beautiful and as resonant as ever of a past she could almost reach out and touch, it was as if a light had gone out of the place. At least she didn't have any more episodes of vertigo in the garden or her room. As Paolo's tan deepened from playing out-doors and his command of Italian became ever more pro-ficient, no word came from the dark-eyed man who haunted

Laura's thoughts. She was forced to concede that, insofar as avoiding entanglements with him, she'd gotten her wish.

A few bright spots brought her comfort. Cristina didn't darken the villa's doorway again. And Stefano didn't seem bothered by his father's generosity in including another outsider in his will. With Enzo gone, he seemed to relax, even to behave in an open, friendly manner toward her. It's as if he wants me to realize there was nothing personal about his actions the night he spied on us, she thought one afternoon as she sat in the villa garden finishing the design for a silk organza dress with a matching neck ruffle that she'd borrowed from her Renaissance musings. There isn't much doubt Enzo and Enzo alone was the object of any harassment he intended.

Their visits to Umberto continued as before. Despite her persistent disapproval of the way he'd behaved toward Guy, Laura found herself liking the gruff but whimsical auto magnate a little more with every day that passed. In many ways, he was Enzo at his worst *and* his best—both irascible and loving, a man intent on having his way, one who was willing to ride roughshod over others' wishes to get it.

That last doesn't describe Enzo, Laura conceded as she sat sketching in the window seat while Umberto and Paolo played checkers. He's much more complicated than his father. And infinitely more generous.

She sensed he was also riddled with self-doubt—troubled by mood swings and apprehensions he didn't feel free to share with her. Though she'd soon be back in her everyday life, beyond the reach of whatever disaster they might have created together, she longed to know what was troubling him. After meeting him, she feared, though a kiss was the most intimate contact they'd likely ever achieve, other men would disappoint.

They were down to four days in Italy and counting when Umberto's lawyer, Dino Lucchanti, drove out from Turin so that the auto magnate could sign his new will in its final version. Appearing shortly after breakfast, Lucchanti spent an estimated twenty minutes in Umberto's room. Afterward, Laura and Paolo paid his grandfather their usual morning visit. From what she could tell, Umberto was in a pensive mood, too tired to cope with Paolo's bouncy, energetic chatter and constant movement.

"Maybe we ought to let you rest a little this morning, Signor Rossi," she suggested, corraling her effusive youngster with a hug.

To her surprise, though Umberto usually insisted he was on the mend and ready for anything, he didn't demur. "Call me Father," he insisted as they started out the door, his head sinking back on the pillow. "You're like a daughter to me now... Guy's ambassador to my sickbed."

That night, she was awakened by the sound of running feet. "What's wrong?" she asked, poking her head into the hallway as Margherita emerged from Umberto's room. "Is Signor Rossi all right?"

The housekeeper-cook was clearly shaken. "He's taken a turn for the worse," she said hoarsely, wiping her eyes with one corner of the apron she'd donned haphazardly over her nightgown. "Signora Emilia has sent for the doctor and Signor Enzo. She, Signora Anna and Signor Stefano are with him. Oh, Signora Laura...he's struggling for every breath. It just breaks my heart. This time, I don't think he's going to make it."

Despite everything his physician could do, the man who had guided the fortunes of Rossi Motorworks in its heyday and made Laura's son, Paolo, an equal heir to the family millions on his last full day of existence in the world, died at 4:27 a.m., an hour almost to the minute after his son Enzo reached his side. Pacing aimlessly in the *sala* in her robe and slippers, Laura glanced up as Enzo came down the stairs.

"He's gone, isn't he?" she asked in response to the look on his face.

Hollow-eyed, disheveled, sporting an overnight growth of beard, Enzo nodded. "He hated lying in bed for hours on end, just waiting for another stroke to happen. It's better this way."

"I'm so very sorry...."

Standing there in faded jeans, a polo shirt and shabby, worn-out loafers on the *sala*'s black-and-white marble tiles, he continued to look at her. "I know you are," he said.

A moment later she was in his arms and his tears were wetting her shoulder. Go ahead, *cry...* that's what you're supposed to do, she urged him with silent ferocity.

At last a door shut upstairs and there were footsteps. Raising his tear-stained face and stepping back from her a little, Enzo gripped Laura's hands. "Your plane ticket's for Friday," he said urgently, crushing her fingers. "Promise me you won't leave."

He hadn't specified how long he expected her to stay. Yet how could she refuse him? He *needed* her. It was as simple as that. For the moment, it would be enough.

"I promise," she answered, knowing that, even as she spoke, the centuries' old connection she'd gravitated toward, feared and attempted so clumsily to avert was weaving itself around them like a straitjacket made of steel cobwebs.

Though the footsteps were Emilia's, and she would reach them in another moment, Enzo tugged her close.

Chapter Seven

Laura's sense of an impending disaster she and Enzo were doomed to recreate returned full-force as Umberto's memorial service approached. By opening her arms to him the night of his father's death, she believed, she'd brought the likelihood of that outcome a little closer. Yet she couldn't force herself to turn her back on him. He counted on their closeness now. He'd made that clear to her. He expected her to stay until Umberto was laid to rest. Though officially her departure for the States had been postponed, not canceled, she had a strong feeling that something else would happen to keep her in Italy once the funeral was past.

Without really intending to, she managed to betray her uneasiness to Carol when she phoned to say Umberto had died and announce that her return would be delayed for another week.

"What's wrong?" her business partner asked at once. "You don't sound like yourself. You can't be grieving for Guy's father. You haven't known him long enough."

Holding the receiver to her ear in Enzo's book-lined study, Laura wished she could couch the thoughts that plagued her in a form that would make at least partial sense. To her frustration, she found she couldn't. To assert she'd known Enzo for centuries, and that trouble might have followed them from a long-ago time and place, would make it sound as if she were going around the bend. She didn't want Carol fretting over her.

"I'm not plunged into sorrow, if that's what you mean," she confessed, "though, to my surprise, I'd begun to like Umberto quite a bit. I'm not sure I can explain."

Though she was a practical soul, Carol could be amazingly intuitive. "Your current state of mind doesn't have anything to do with your brother-in-law, does it?" she asked speculatively. "Or a continuation of those dizzy spells you suffered at home?"

The satellite phone connection was empty of conversation for a moment. "It might," Laura conceded, deliberately vague about which question she was answering.

"You've had more of them? The dizzy spells, I mean?"

She hated to admit the truth. But she supposed she might as well. Carol had probably guessed anyway.

"There've been two," she acknowledged. "The most recent was more than a week ago. I'm hoping I've seen the last of them."

Carol responded that she hoped so, too. "The minute you get home, I want you to consult a doctor," she said. "You might even consider seeing one in Italy, depending on how long you plan to be there. Meanwhile, take it easy, all right? Don't skip any meals. And get plenty of rest."

"I will," Laura promised.

Transatlantic calls didn't come cheap, and they ended the conversation rather quickly after that, without returning to the topic of Enzo, and Laura's feelings for him. It was just as well. Walking into the room as she hung up the phone, he put his arms around her.

"Thank heaven for you, *cara,*" he murmured, resting his cheek against her hair. "You're an island of repose in the midst of wrangling."

If the Rossis are arguing, Paolo and I are likely at the heart of it, Laura thought. I want to go home. Simultaneously she felt the bond between her and Enzo deepening.

The *uffizio dei morti* or formal burial service of Umberto Amadeo Rossi, famed sports car designer, wealthy industrialist and erstwhile paparazzi target, thanks to his colorful personality and numerous affairs of the heart— several of them involving well-known film stars—was held at Turin's Duomo, otherwise known as the Cathedral of the Holy Shroud. It had rained that morning, and the sky was like lead. As the cortege drew up, the downpour began anew. The square in front of the cathedral bloomed with black umbrellas like flowers opening in time-lapse photography.

Smelling of dust, sanctity and hothouse flowers, the Duomo's gloomy, echoing interior did little to lighten an already somber mood. Laura had expected a sizable outpouring of sympathy and respect for her late father-in-law. Nonetheless, she was slightly taken aback by the number of celebrities, business executives and government officials who crowded into the nave alongside employees from the Rossi assembly line and neighbors of the Villa Voglia estate. To control the curious and restrain potential troublemakers, police had cordoned off the Duomo's numerous entrances. Still, the family was forced to run a gauntlet of reporters, photographers and TV cameramen on their way from limousine to church.

To their distinct displeasure, Cristina, Vittorio and their son, 'Nardo, were relegated to the second row. Seated beside Anna in front of them, Laura could feel the knife-thrust of her sister-in-law's jealousy between her shoulder blades. Enzo and Emilia asked that I sit here, she defended herself silently. Surely you don't expect me to upset them for your sake.

Her hand resting lightly on Enzo's arm, the Rossi matriarch stared straight ahead, her eyes like shuttered windows. She seemed to draw strength from him, and from Paolo, whom she'd insisted must sit at her right hand. Dressed in a dark gray suit and miniature tie that had been hastily ordered for him from Enzo's tailor in Milan, Laura's little boy was silent, solemn and, for once, completely biddable. His blond hair shone like an angel's in the filtered light from the cathedral windows.

Shortly after it had occurred, Laura had attempted to answer Paolo's questions about his grandfather's death. "He's with your daddy in heaven," she'd told him. "They were angry at each other when they were both alive. But now they're friends. Heaven is a wonderful place."

Frowning, Paolo had considered her remarks for a moment. "It's nice here, too, Mommy," he'd asserted in the skeptical tone he adopted whenever her explanations failed to satisfy him. "I wish they'd stayed longer. Will they come back to see us someday?"

"No, sweetheart." She'd shaken her head. "Not in the way you mean."

That wasn't much of an answer, she thought, gazing at Umberto's casket, which was half hidden beneath its massive spray of lilies. But it was the best one I could give. To tell him what I'm beginning to think would only confuse him.

During the final days of his life, Umberto's chief delight had been their visits. Ill as he'd been, he'd told Paolo stories about his youth and expended the effort to teach him how to cheat at checkers. Picturing him as he must look now, waxen and cold inside his expensive coffin, was almost enough to convince her that earthly life was over when the last breath left the body. But not quite. Since coming face-to-face with the Renaissance nobleman's portrait and glimpsing what appeared to be the shadowy images of revels in a bygone day, she'd begun to wonder if there was more to each person's existence than the available evidence could substantiate.

I've beheld what appear to be windows between past and present, though my vision has been faulty, she thought as the Duomo choir began to sing the Dies Irae with poignant grace. If they exist, then reincarnation might be possible, as well. Maybe the heaven I described to Paolo as such a permanent place is in reality a leaky boat, and we *can* come back. Begin anew. Gravitate to former enemies and lovers.

The notion didn't allay her fears. On the contrary, they intensified. If affinity and passion could bridge the abyss of years, why not jealousy? And hatred? What if danger and evildoing lurked as the centuries unfolded, awaiting a familiar configuration of souls to reassert itself? It had occurred to her in the small hours of several restless nights that, together, she and Enzo might form part of such a configuration.

Following the reading, Enzo mounted to a special microphone placed at the communion rail to give the eulogy. Husky with loss, his voice washed over Laura in waves, subduing the watchdog at her heart's gate. I belong with him, she admitted, little shivers of fatalism cascading down her spine. *And it's nothing new*. Whatever is fated to happen is already happening.

At last the service was over. Umberto's coffin was loaded into a shiny black hearse for the trip back to the Villa Voglia, where he would be interred near the private chapel at the garden's edge. Their faces veiled, their expensive mourning clothes unrelieved by the gleam of gold or mitigating color, the Rossi women were helped by ushers into limousines. Their men followed. Seated beside Laura as they moved through city streets and gained the countryside, Sofia wept noisily into a lace-edged handkerchief.

The graveside formalities beside the little-used stone chapel on the villa property seemed endless from Laura's point of view. Usurping the role of principal mourner, Emilia continued to claim the support of Enzo and Paolo, leaving Laura to hold Anna's hand. For some reason, Cristina seemed to be giving her mother the cold shoulder. *I wonder if Anna defended Paolo's right to inherit?* Laura thought. *And earned her daughter's contempt?*

Finally the last prayer had been said, the last handful of Villa Voglia earth flung on Umberto's coffin lid. Turning away from the gravesite, where old Michele and one of the estate laborers would complete the job they'd started, they proceeded into the house. After a brief pause to freshen up, they received guests in the *sala,* greeting those friends of the family and relatives who'd been invited to accompany the casket down to the country for burial, and accepting lengthy condolences. Introduced to all and sundry as "Guy's widow," Laura found herself discussing the tragedy of his death, as well as Umberto's, with a succession of total strangers. Though she wasn't grieving for Guy any longer, the memory of his accident was still fraught with pain for her. The result was a splitting headache. Her discomfort was only increased by the belligerent looks Cristina continued to fling in her direction.

Finally she'd had enough. "I'm not feeling well," she whispered to Gemma, who was serving coffee from a silver urn. "Tell Signora Emilia I've gone upstairs to lie down a while. And keep an eye on Paolo for me, please."

The murmurs of Umberto's funeral guests receded as she climbed the north staircase and reached the upstairs hall. *How familiar their voices sound,* she thought. *I wonder* what they remind me of. A party I attended in my college days?

Moments later, as she walked into the high-ceilinged room that she'd begun to think of as hers, reality stumbled. The lights and colors of her surroundings threatened to fragment, and a dizzy spell to assert itself. Somehow she managed to retain control, to push back the veils of illusion until they dispersed, like cobwebs. *I should have eaten something,* she thought. *Brought one of Margherita's tea cakes upstairs wrapped in a napkin.*

Distractedly massaging her temples, she stepped out of her high heels, stripped off the black silk jacket dress of her own design that Carol had air-expressed her from Chicago. Wearing just her slip, she turned back the coverlet and top sheet on her old-fashioned canopied bed. *A nap between cool sheets will do me good,* she thought, letting weariness claim her. *I don't have to make any decisions about going home until I'm rested.*

That morning, during a brief encounter in the breakfast room, where they'd gone to fortify themselves for the day with black coffee and anise-flavored toast, the dark-haired scion of the Rossi family had urged her to remain in Italy for the reading of his father's will. According to him, it was scheduled to take place in Dino Lucchanti's Turin law office two weeks hence.

"Dino assures me Cristina and Vittorio won't be able to overturn the will," he'd told her. "Still, it might be wise to attend, and represent Paolo's interests."

It's possible Paolo's best interests—and mine—would be served by returning to America at once, she'd thought, declining to give him an answer. *I didn't come here to battle Cristina. Or for monetary gain.* Even as her feelings for Enzo continued to deepen, the urge to avoid catastrophe by running from him while she could was gathering strength.

She'd neglected to shut her door to the hall completely, and she glanced up to find Enzo standing there. "Gemma said you weren't feeling well," he reported, running his eyes over the curves so sinuously revealed by her clinging undergarment.

He looked so intense in his dark suit—like her Renaissance nobleman. And so needful of human contact. She wanted to make his hurt go away, to nestle in his arms.

"I have a headache," she answered, declining to snatch up a robe for modesty's sake.

He knew what headaches were like. Whenever he spent time at the villa, his migraines got worse. The same thing was true of his nightmares.

"Can I get you something?" he asked.

"No. I'll be all right."

Seconds later, they were clinging together as if drawn by a powerful magnet. How delectable, how life-giving, she is! he thought. A refuge from black moods and loneliness. "You're thinking of going back, despite our talk this morning...aren't you?" he said, daring to run his hands over her lower back and the upper curve of her buttocks through her slip's satiny fabric.

Though it was a day for mourning and circumspection, desire sang like a chorus of sirens in her blood. She nodded, not trusting herself to speak.

"Stay," he urged. "If not for Paolo's sake, because I want you to. I'll be with you here at the villa as often as my responsibilities permit."

A fruit on a bent branch, dangling beyond her reach, escape retreated. Uncharacteristic but frequent since her journey into metaphysical questioning and half-perceived visions had begun, a sense of fatalism washed over her. She knew she'd continue to play her role in their strangely familiar pas de deux for a little while yet.

"All right," she said.

His relief cresting like a wave, he tightened his grip. "Though we've just buried my father, I have to fly to Rome tomorrow on business," he admitted regretfully. "I'll be back Wednesday. It may sound mercenary, but I need to escape my grief for him ... the atmosphere of loss that will permeate this house. Say you'll leave Paolo in my mother's care and come to Turin with me overnight. If you like, we can tour the fabric houses. The contacts you make will be invaluable to you professionally."

Much as the idea of familiarizing herself with Italian methods of fabric production appealed to her, Laura regarded the suggestion as a form of bribery, a convenient excuse he'd concocted in order to spirit her away from the Villa Voglia. It would be dangerous to go away with him when you're already half besotted and nothing can come of it, her sensible side pointed out. Maybe so, her more willful self argued, but once you leave, it'll be years before you see him again.

She supposed Anna wouldn't mind. Unless she missed her guess, her somewhat mousy but sweet-tempered mother-in-law had done the lion's share of her grieving for Umberto many years earlier. She'd probably be delighted to be put in temporary charge of her grandson.

"I *would* like to see how Italian weavers work, how the patterns are designed and the dye lots batched," she decided, flushed at her complicity. "I'll ask your mother to watch Paolo for me as soon as I have a chance."

The kiss he feathered on her mouth before leaving her to her rest temporarily banished scruples and premonitions from her head.

Most of the guests had gone by the time Laura awoke and sought her mother-in-law downstairs. As she'd hoped, Anna was happy to grant her request. "I probably shouldn't talk this way on the day my husband is buried," Anna admitted with a rueful smile, "but Paolo and I will have a wonderful time together. Surely you realize, Laura, what a great comfort he is to us."

Not to Cristina, Laura thought. Or her cardboard yesman husband. Thanking Anna and giving her a daughterly hug, she slipped into Enzo's study to use the phone. Given the six-hour time difference between Turin and Chicago, Carol would be at her desk. I doubt she'll be happy when she hears what I have to say, Laura thought. By lingering in Italy, I'll be putting next fall's schedule in jeopardy.

To her surprise, her partner was more understanding than she had any right to expect. Anticipating another delay, she'd hired a student from the Art Institute to "clean up" the rough designs Laura had completed before her departure so that they could be submitted to the pattern-maker. Her eminent reasonableness evoked a guilty flood of reassurances from Laura's lips.

"I'll be back by the twentieth, come hell or high water," Laura vowed. "In fact, I plan to return home immediately after our meeting in the lawyer's office. I feel awful sticking you with so much work in the meantime. Yet I agree with Enzo... Paolo's interests should be protected."

At the breakfast table the following morning, Cristina was frowning, tight-lipped. Despite Emilia's absence, however, she didn't let her resentment spill over. It was only when Gemma delivered a phone message from the airline confirming Laura's change of schedule that the volatile brunette's self-control evaporated.

"Interesting, isn't it?" she said to no one in particular, employing a cutting tone. "She plans to leave the minute she has what she came for... a sizable chunk of 'Nardo's inheritance. Never mind that she took advantage of Father's illness, and promised him she and her brat would remain in

Italy. He's gone now. He can't hold her to it. Well, Vittorio and I aren't going to let her get away with it...."

With a rush of adrenaline, Laura saw red. Cristina had listened in on her call. "I never made any such promise, nor did your father ask me to!" she retorted angrily. "How dare you impugn my motives? Or suggest I took advantage of Umberto? I came to heal a family wound, not for your precious Rossi money. The fact is, I don't need it! I have a life and a career...something you know nothing about!"

Laura flung down her napkin and quit the breakfast room. She would have called the airlines on the spot and ordered tickets for that afternoon if Enzo hadn't followed her and argued that she was playing into his sister's hands.

"Paolo has every right to be included in his grandfather's will," he insisted, "just as Guy did. Besides, I need you. I don't want you to go before we can spend some time together."

Cristina left for Turin a few minutes before Enzo's departure for the airport. Uninterested in the controversy over her father's will—or much of anything else that went on at Villa Voglia, apparently—Sofia came downstairs after everyone had left the table to avail herself of black coffee and a quick glance at the morning paper. She pointed the nose of her Rossi sedan, the twin of Cristina's, toward San Remo an hour later without saying more than the briefest of goodbyes to anyone.

That left Laura, Paolo, Anna, Stefano and Emilia holding down the fort. A feeling of emptiness, of a vacuum waiting to be filled, seemed to descend on the lovely old villa and its grounds, evoked by the void of Umberto's absence and Emilia's wish that she not be disturbed. Controlled and private in her sorrow for the sixty-seven-year-old man whom she'd still thought of as her child, the bereaved matriarch had shut herself up in her second-floor suite to go through old photographs of Umberto as a boy and newspaper clippings that depicted his many triumphs.

The autumn weather had turned glorious, as if to mock the prevailing mood. By the time Wednesday rolled around, Laura was too filled with restless energy to work on her designs. Preoccupied with the thought of Enzo's return, she took Paolo for a walk. They'd gone only a short distance toward the nearest patch of woods, where they planned to hunt for wildflowers, when they came across Michele and his prized mongrel dog. Dressed in baggy pants, a worn corduroy shirt and a battered cap, the old gardener was carrying a staff and a disreputable-looking burlap bag, which appeared to be empty. He was headed for the woods, too.

"Out for a stroll?" Laura asked.

Michele smiled his gap-toothed smile. "No, *signora*. We seek truffles. The food of heaven. It's possible in the fall to find them in these woods. Old Cesare, here, he's the expert. You and your boy... you're welcome to come along."

Having tasted truffles on her first day in Italy, Laura knew he wasn't exaggerating. They really were heavenly. Delighted by his offer, she accepted. Swinging Paolo's hand in hers, she fell into step with the gardener as he proceeded down the winding dirt path. Somewhere, a bird chirped. Light filtered between the trees. It had rained during the night, and the ground was soft. Leaves and leaf mold lay in thick layers underfoot.

"This looks like as good a place as any to let Cesare follow his nose," Michele said at last, untying the frayed lead rope from his dog's collar and giving him his head.

A white mutt of indeterminate age with liverish brown spots and floppy, moth-eaten looking ears, Cesare seemed to know what was expected of him. As Laura and Paolo watched, he took off at once, whining, sniffing and run-

ning in what appeared to be an aimless zigzag pattern
through the leaves and underbrush. Before long, though, he
seemed to have located what he was looking for. His sniffing narrowed to a particular spot, and he began to dig in
earnest.

Michele didn't let him complete the task. Pulling a small
trowel and a dog treat from his pants pocket, he gave the
latter to Cesare and carefully completed the digging with the
former. A short time later, he held a pale, earth-stained tu-
ber aloft in triumph. To Laura, who had never smelled the
much-sought-after delicacy fresh from the earth before, its
aroma was indescribable—loamy, garlicky, and utterly
mouth-watering.

"The white truffle of Piemonte," Michele said with a
grin. "He brings many lire in the Alba market."

The gardener's bag held a respectable collection of truffles, and Paolo had managed to get himself thoroughly
filthy playing among the leaves, when they heard the dull
thud of a horse's hooves. Seconds later, a dark-haired rider
came into view.

Enzo! He's back early! Laura thought with a surge of
pleasure, somewhat surprised that he'd come looking for
them on horseback. Since her arrival at the Villa Voglia, he
hadn't gone near the stable. She hadn't guessed he was interested in equestrian pursuits.

A moment later, she realized with a little frisson of dis-
appointment that she'd been mistaken. The rider in nut-
brown corduroy trousers and fraying gray sweater who
cantered to a halt beside them was not Enzo, but Stefano—
the half brother he couldn't abide.

At close hand, the resemblance wasn't that remarkable.
Yet she could see how she'd made the error. Like Enzo,
Stefano was middling tall, and dark. At a certain angle, in
just the right light, the brothers bore each other a marked
family resemblance. As she stood looking up at him, a

dream fragment tugged at her, so transitory she couldn't place it. The words "Not him . . . *me*" drifted through her head.

"I'm on my way back to the villa," Stefano said with his twisted grin. "If you're heading in that direction, I'd be happy to give you a lift."

She wasn't sure if he was joking or serious. "I don't think . . ."

Paolo tugged at her with grubby hands. "Please, Mommy!" he begged. "Say yes. I want to ride him."

Her little boy was too small, the mare's back too high and her temperament too uncertain for Laura to let him have his way. What if he fell off . . . broke a leg?

"I'll dismount . . . put Paolo in the saddle. We can lead the mare at a slow walk," Stefano offered, as if she'd articulated her objections.

The plan seemed innocuous enough. Pausing to thank Michele for taking them along on his truffle hunt, Laura allowed Stefano to lift Paolo into the mare's saddle in his place. With the family outsider holding the reins, they started back toward the villa, proceeding slowly so that Paolo wouldn't lose his grip.

They had just emerged from the woods and were heading for the vine-clad stable when Enzo's Rossi convertible appeared in the drive. Catching sight of them, he veered in their direction. "What have we here . . . a horseback-riding lesson?" he asked, sounding less than pleased, as he slowed to a crawl beside them.

It wasn't the homecoming scene Laura had pictured. She suppressed an urge to apologize. By allowing Stefano to give Paolo a horseback ride, she hadn't done anything so terrible, in her opinion.

"We were truffle hunting with Michele in the woods, and Stefano offered Paolo a ride home," she explained, a trifle resentfully.

His eyes unreadable behind dark sunglasses, Enzo glanced at his half brother as if to appraise his motives. "Don't let me interrupt," he said at last with marked irritation of his own, returning his gaze to her. "I'll see you later, at the house."

Though she couldn't have said why, she sensed Stefano was pleased by the interchange. His shoulders lifted in a deprecating little shrug as Enzo backed up his powerful sports car and drove off in the direction of the villa turnaround. Whatever he was thinking, she felt certain, it wasn't flattering.

While Laura sat moodily on a bale of hay in the estate's ancient, vine-clad stable, waiting for Paolo to finish helping Stefano groom and water his mare, Enzo went upstairs to pay his respects to his grandmother. At his knock, she bade him enter. Clad in a black silk dress that emphasized her thinness and sallow complexion, the Rossi matriarch was seated in her favorite straight-backed armchair, beside a table laden with photographs of her son, Umberto. With the subtlety of a sigh, a stray breeze stirred the curtains that hid her balcony from view.

"Are you all right, Grandmother?" he asked.

She nodded. "Pull up a chair, Enzo. I want to talk to you."

Beginning ambiguously enough with an observation that the Villa Voglia wouldn't be the same without Paolo, she repeated her theory that he must marry Laura to keep the boy in Italy.

"He's all we have left of Guy," she said, her dark eyes glittering. "Unless you produce a son, he's the only viable heir of his generation we shall have to command the family fortunes and oversee Rossi Motorworks."

Too well he knew Emilia's opinion of 'Nardo. The truth was, he shared it. The boy was gluttonous, deceitful and ill-

tempered. To complicate matters, Cristina's doctors had
told her she mustn't have another baby. Meanwhile, the
thought of having Laura for his wife struck a deeply resonant chord within him.

"What you're suggesting is outrageous, Grandmother,"
he said, when she gave him an opportunity to speak. "The
kind of marriage you're talking about went out with the last
century."

Emilia knew him like a book, and that afternoon she
proved it. "You haven't said *no*," she pointed out. "Perhaps it wouldn't be such a sacrifice. Think about it, *caro*.
Laura may be a businesswoman and an American, with
strong ties to her native country. But she belongs here at the
villa. I sensed that from the moment I set eyes on her."

Supper was a quiet affair, with Emilia putting in her first
appearance at the table since Umberto's funeral. As she
nibbled at *grissini* and watched Enzo eat his salad, Laura
wondered if he was still annoyed at having found her in
Stefano's company when he returned from Rome. Surprisingly, he didn't seem to be. Yet he'd barely spoken to her.
Did he mean it when he said we'd spend a night together in
Turin? she thought. Or has he changed his mind?

At the conclusion of the meal, Gemma offered to read
Paolo a story, bathe him and put him to bed. Her generosity left Laura at loose ends. If Enzo ignores me...shuts
himself up in his office...I'll invade his privacy, she
thought. Have it out with him.

He didn't. Instead, as they left the dining room, he invited her to take the evening air. Tucking her hand in the
curve of his arm, he led her down the steps past the fountain to a little copse of cypresses that sheltered a carved stone
bench.

"Shall we?" he asked, dusting off the seat.

She shook her head. "I'd rather walk a little."

His dark eyes studied her. "What's the matter, Laura?"

"Nothing." She was silent a moment. "Aren't we going to Turin, the way you said?"

The corners of his mouth curved. She *wanted* to go with him. For that moment, at least, the negative emotions that vexed him seemed as frangible, as lacking in substance, as mist or smoke. "I propose we leave in the morning," he responded, "if that's all right with you."

The soft parting of her lips was answer enough. He couldn't stop himself from lowering his mouth to kiss them.

So quickly it almost took her breath away, their feelings spiraled out of control. Invading her moist privacy, Enzo's tongue threatened to sear her very soul. A pit of longing opened between her legs, throbbing with her need for him. I want him there, she thought helplessly. Taking complete possession. Filling me to bursting. Never, not even in her most abandoned moments with Guy, had she wanted a man so much.

From a window on the villa's second floor, Stefano was watching them. An hour or so later, after she'd parted from Enzo with flushed cheeks at the foot of the *sala*'s north stairs, he rapped lightly at the door to her room.

"Stefano... what is it?" she demanded in surprise when she opened it to find him standing there.

"May I speak with you a moment?"

She didn't want her mood destroyed. Or Enzo to find him in her company. Yet he was Paolo's uncle, Guy's and Enzo's half brother. He'd been friendly, even cordial, to them that afternoon. Suppressing a grimace of reluctance, she stepped aside, leaving the door open. "What's this about?" she asked.

Stefano didn't pull any punches. "I saw you and Enzo kissing in the garden," he said. "No... let me finish. I like you, Laura. And I think I ought to warn you. My half brother has a mistress in the Lake District . . . someone he's known for years. Getting involved with him would be a mistake."

By sheer force of will, Laura kept the sinking feeling that attacked the pit of her stomach from registering on her face. "What happened between me and Enzo in the garden is none of your affair," she retorted coldly. "I'll be returning to the States soon. That ought to put your fears to rest."

Stefano continued to regard her appraisingly. She had the sudden notion he'd romance her himself if he dared, if only to make Enzo jealous.

"In the meantime," he advised, "I'd be careful, if I were you. His temper is infamous . . . prone to erupt without warning, particularly when he's here at the estate. Given the stress caused by our father's death, I can't imagine how he's kept it under control so long."

Uncertain how to respond, Laura stared at him in consternation.

Shrugging, as if to turn away, Stefano fired a parting shot. "There was an accident," he disclosed, "involving Enzo and his former fiancée. They were arguing while traveling at a high rate of speed. He wrenched the steering wheel from her grasp. Both were seriously injured. Look at him closely . . . near his hairline, at the temples. You can still see the scars."

By now, Laura wasn't just irritated. She was thoroughly furious. She hated the feeling of collusion their enforced tête-à-tête gave her, the seeds of distrust he'd planted in her head. "What about the scar on *your* cheek?" she snapped. "Did you get it in a fight?"

"How strange you should ask," Stefano replied with an air of calm that only upset her further. "Enzo gave it to me with a horsewhip when we were seventeen . . . the year I came to live at the Villa Voglia."

Chapter Eight

Her sleeves fluttering and her hair blowing freely in his open sports car as Enzo drove them to Turin the following morning, Laura tried not to let Stefano's comments affect her too much. You've heard one side of the story, she reminded herself. That's all. It's clear that, as the family outsider, Stefano's extremely jealous. Yet she couldn't put the conversation out of her head. Disturbing as his allegations about Enzo's temper had been, her personal knowledge of the dark-haired man who'd escorted her to Italy tended to refute them somewhat. It was Stefano's talk of a mistress in the Lake District that reverberated uncomfortably in her thoughts, weaving itself in unpleasant counterpoint to their sporadic dialogue as they sped toward their destination.

When they reached the city, Enzo took her to the fabric houses first. Thanks to his excellent connections, they were admitted as honored guests and given the grand tour. At her favorite, Affianza Silks, a branch of the famed parent company in Como, she watched dense paisleys acquire their

pattern, luscious silk twills emerge from the dye vats, moires
and jacquards take shape on a seventy-five-thousand-dollar
Dornier loom capable of weaving eighty meters of cloth
daily. The *cucina colori* or color kitchen, where dyes were
mixed in quantities as exacting as 0.1 gram, utterly fascinated her.

Though she'd have preferred to lunch alone with Enzo in
some intimate little bistro, she didn't feel she could turn
down an invitation from Gianfranca Morelli, Affianza's
production coordinator, to dine in the firm's executive suite.
Over Barolo wine, salad and *tagliatelle* tossed with vegeta-
ble strips, basil and tomato, she, Enzo and Signorina
Morelli discussed the current worries in the silk trade—union contracts, Korean competition, a declining market for
top-quality fabric.

"We're still first in printing intricate designs," their
hostess said as coffee was served. "The Koreans haven't
mastered the art of perfect registration with as many as fifty
screens. But they're gaining on us. If you like, Signora
Rossi, we'll put you on our sample list. We can weave to order...create special patterns to carry out the theme of a
collection. And we can most certainly use the business."

Throughout the meal, Enzo was charming company.
Away from the villa, he didn't seem so distracted. He didn't
massage the bridge of his nose as if he were coming down
with a headache. Perhaps because his father had been sick
so long, he didn't seem to find it difficult to set his grief
aside and participate fully in the conversation.

As a result, she was seized with apprehension when she
saw his brow furrow later that afternoon as they toured a
special exhibit of sixteenth-century paintings in a gallery in
a small palazzo near the Duomo. Several paces ahead of her
as she lingered over a miniature gem of a landscape, he
halted before a gilt-framed portrait. When she joined him,
she was quickly frowning, too. Mesmerized and chilled, she

stared at the likeness of a dark-haired churchman clad in the scarlet robes of a cardinal.

His was the face she'd sketched at the Art Institute. And yet it wasn't. Could he be the same subject, painted twenty years later? If so, her supremely masculine, intense nobleman had renounced wealth and the pleasures of the body, dedicated his life to the church. The thought saddened her, even as she shivered at the changes in him. The lines that had appeared in his face weren't pretty. His years as a religious hadn't been kind to him.

At the very least, the man who gazed at them from the present canvas and her Renaissance courtier were twins, she felt certain. If they were one and the same, she was puzzled by her feelings. Before the earlier portrait, she'd felt recognition, a reluctant fascination. By contrast, her emotions when she gazed at the current portrait were fear and uneasiness.

I hope to God I don't embarrass myself and have one of my dizzy spells with Enzo looking on, she thought, digging her nails into her palms as a way of keeping focused. Mercifully, none seemed to be in the offing. She prayed the foreboding of danger or disaster to come that strengthened as she gazed into the churchman's painted eyes was a figment of her imagination.

"Who *was* he, anyway?" she asked shakily after a moment, trusting herself sufficiently to squint at the accompanying card, which had been printed in small italic type and affixed to the wall beside the portrait.

"Giulio Cardinal Uccelli." Enzo's voice had a slight edge to it.

She stopped attempting to read the museum label. "I get the impression you've heard of him before. He doesn't exactly look like a saint. Was he a villain of some sort?"

The question seemed to relax him a little, though his frown remained in place. "Not that I know of," he said. "I admit he doesn't look like the most pleasant sort. Actually, there's a remote blood tie between the Uccelli and Rossi families. The Uccellis built the Villa Voglia in the early fifteen-hundreds. It was sold later that century, when the male line died out. Perhaps because of the connection I mentioned, my great-grandfather bought the property for use as a country home in the late nineteenth century."

Enzo's matter-of-fact tone notwithstanding, goose bumps prickled Laura's arms. "Do you know if he had a brother?" she asked.

The query was enough of a non sequitur that Enzo gave her a somewhat startled look. "As a matter of fact, he did," he replied. "According to my grandmother, the cardinal's older brother, who inherited the villa, was the last Uccelli. The cardinal, too... presumably... was childless. We Rossis are peripherally descended from their sister, who married a Milanese nobleman."

Enzo's mood seemed to lighten when they left the gallery a short time later. Buoyed though she was, Laura continued thinking about the cardinal and her Renaissance nobleman. I can't believe they're one and the same, she thought. I had a strong feeling of empathy, even attraction, toward the latter, whereas the churchman, with his sinister, knowing looks, caused a sliver of uneasiness to pierce my heart.

She was also highly cognizant of the passing hours. Her time alone with Enzo would be limited, and she was determined to make the most of it. Whatever connection might exist between herself, the nobleman and the cardinal, she didn't know how to unravel it. She'd deliberately put it out of her thoughts.

Following an afternoon spent touring the city and strolling its broad, French-influenced boulevards, they stopped at the Palazzo Rossi to freshen up and change before going out to eat. Having deposited her overnight bag in the guest room she and Paolo had used so briefly on their first day in Italy, Laura took a quick shower and slipped into the black dress she'd worn to Umberto's funeral. Minus its jacket, which had fitted it for that somber occasion, it was alluring in the extreme. Thin straps meticulously appliquéd with tiny silver flowers, beads and sequins held up a deeply décolleté bodice. The narrow silken skirt slid like a caress over her hips, emphasizing their slender but rounded shape.

The success of her choice was reflected in Enzo's face when they met a few minutes later in his eclectic, stylish living room. "*Cara...* you look good enough to eat," he said, lightly running his hands down her bare arms as his eyes took in every detail of her appearance. "What do you say we stay here...skip dinner? At the very least, have dessert first?"

The comment catapulted them into the state of tingling anticipation they'd shared in the villa garden, when he'd kissed her there so passionately the night before. Tonight, the feeling was even more intense. Will we become lovers? Laura wondered, vibrating at his touch. Everything augurs it. We're alone. His apartment is at our disposal. Stefano can't spy on us. Even the fact that they'd soon be an ocean apart, with the most infrequent of chances to see each other, militated in that direction. It was a now-or-never situation.

What was life if you never took a risk?

"I happen to love dessert," she responded, allowing her gaze to drown in his as she bought them an hour or two to let their imagination run wild. "But isn't antipasto traditional? Doesn't it whet the appetite?"

Dinner at Cambio, a luxurious restaurant situated in an old palazzo decorated with crystal chandeliers, Austrian damask shades and fresh flowers atop snowy tablecloths, was both elegant and intimate. In full view of their waiter, who wore the traditional long white apron over his formal garb, they gazed sensuously and deeply at each other.

Swayed by her fantasy about what would happen when they returned to his apartment, Laura was almost too excited to taste her *vitello tonnato* and fresh salmon steak.

In view of her earlier remark, Enzo wouldn't let her get by with skipping dessert. "Everything about this evening must be perfect," he insisted as their smiling server waited beside his trolley of sweets. "That means a bite of Cambio's famous chocolate cake, at least."

Encouraged to take risks, she proposed they share a slice. Eating off the same plate with Enzo was one of the most subtly erotic forms of play she'd ever experienced. With her son in Anna's care and her grief for Guy thoroughly healed, she felt free to imagine them naked, feeding each other tidbits in bed as a prelude to making love. The mental picture caused her nipples to tighten beneath her dress.

At Enzo's suggestion, they walked off their meal in Turin's vast riverside Parco del Valentino, a favorite promenade of lovers, and a jumping-off point for some of the city's liveliest night spots. Noting that he hadn't been dancing for quite some time, with the exception of their turn on the grass at the Villa Voglia, he took her to the African Club, where a reggae band was holding forth. Lilting and energetic, the fast numbers caused their blood to flow more briskly and made them smile at each other. But it was the slow numbers that Laura liked best. We move like one person... as if we'd always danced together, she thought, enjoying Enzo's warmth, his citrus-based scent.

It was after midnight by the time he parked his white sports car in the Palazzo Rossi's cavernous garage and escorted her upstairs to his apartment in its old-fashioned cage elevator. Someone—his unseen houseman, she guessed—had switched on soft lighting in his living room against their return. Subtly the question of whether they'd become lovers reasserted itself.

"How about a nightcap?" Enzo asked.

"All right," she agreed, tossing her black taffeta rain-coat over one of his white upholstered chairs and standing there at loose ends in her beautiful dress.

As she watched, Enzo retrieved a bottle of brandy and Benedictine, plus two cordial glasses, from behind the center doors of his walnut *pietra dura* bookcase. Uncorking the bottle and filling both glasses, he handed one of them to her.

"To us," he said, clicking his against it.

Tingling with her need for him, Laura reciprocated. They sipped at the potent liqueur, their eyes locked in silent communication. I love him, she thought, letting the truth of her feelings slip its leash. I want to bring him ecstasy. Shelter him from every hurt. The fact that their worlds were oceans apart didn't enter into it. Though her premonition of a danger that connected him with her dizzy spells and the two Renaissance-era portraits was as strong as ever, she pushed it from her consciousness.

I'd run any risk just to sleep with him tonight, she admitted to herself. It'll be our only chance. When we return to the villa tomorrow, watchful eyes will follow us. He'll be my brother-in-law. I'll be Paolo's mother. Guy's widow.

It was as if he could follow the trajectory of her thoughts. "Ah, Laura..." he whispered with a shake of his head. Reaching for her drink, he set it aside, along with his, on a nearby table. A moment later, he'd taken her in his arms. Tempted when one of her sequin-embroidered straps slid down her arm, he bent to kiss her naked shoulder. So soft it bordered on a whimper, a moan of pleasure escaped her as he slid one hand up her stocking-clad thigh, hoisting the hem of her dress.

Yes...oh, yes...she breathed, tightening the place within her where she wanted him. I'm ready to merge with you. Clasp you tight. I don't care about tomorrow. Or the disquiet I feel. The sadness that will overwhelm me when it's

time to part. By touching her the way he had, he'd set a fire
to raging.

She almost stumbled when he put her from him and
carefully replaced her strap atop her shoulder. "What...
what's wrong?" she asked.

Enzo spread his hands in an abortive little gesture. How
could he make her understand without explaining what his
life had been? As he'd held her in his arms, he'd thought of
the portrait they'd seen that afternoon and experienced the
first stabbing pains of one of his monster headaches.

"There's a lot I haven't told you about myself," he said,
trying not to let his physical anguish show in his face.

Laura shrugged, ignoring her little stab of fear. "Try me.
I'm a good listener."

Already the pain was mounting, spreading to the top of
his head and the back of his neck. He'd have to take something. He wished to hell he hadn't touched a drop of alco-
hol.

"I'm not sure I feel comfortable putting it into words,"
he admitted. "Or that I ought to burden you with my problems tonight."

If not now, when? Laura demanded silently. If not me,
who? Haven't you guessed how much you mean to me?

I blame myself, Enzo thought. If I hadn't brought her
here, neither of us would be at this juncture. Despite the
pounding in his head, he wanted her so much that he was
aching with it. He just couldn't justify taking what she
might be willing to give. She deserved better—a lover whose
sleep wasn't fraught with nightmares. One without a temper, or debilitating headaches, whose moods were sunny,
complementing hers.

"Surely I don't need to remind you that, because of our
family ties, we can't afford casual sex," he said at last.
"Besides... it's like you told Cristina... you have a career,
a *life,* back in the States."

I don't care about those things tonight, Laura thought. And I don't need any lectures. "I was furious with Cristina," she admitted. "But I didn't mean..."

"You may have been furious. But you spoke the truth."

Pushed past reticence, Laura found herself giving voice to words she'd never planned to speak. "Stefano claims you have a temper," she said in a little rush. "That you and your former fiancée were nearly killed in a car accident because you wrenched the wheel from her in the middle of an argument. Is that the deep, dark secret you're so afraid to air?"

Though Enzo winced at Stefano's tale-bearing, the explosion she expected didn't materialize. Luciana would have plunged the car down that embankment if I hadn't stopped her, he reminded himself. I saved our lives by taking control of the wheel. But it's true... my temper had a lot to do with getting the argument started in the first place.

By now the pain in his head was excruciating. "Stefano is correct," he admitted, privately damning his half brother to hell. "But he doesn't know the half of it. I beg you, Laura. Don't push. God knows I'd like to lay my problems in your lap. Make passionate, sustained love to you. But for tonight, at least, that's out of the question."

Though her lower lip was quivering, Laura's chin had come up a notch. If he's determined to reject me...shut me out, she thought, there's nothing I can do about it. I'll serve my sentence here in Italy until the will is read, then return to Chicago. Once I'm home again, we probably won't see each other for years.

"Have it your way," she said. "If you don't mind, I think I'll say good-night."

He insisted on escorting her to her door, planting a light kiss on her forehead. As she struggled to fall asleep a short time later, tucked between pima cotton sheets in his capacious guest room bed, tears wet her pillow. I don't want things to end this way, she thought. But what choice do I have? The fact that portents of danger had ebbed with their closeness wasn't any comfort.

The digital clock on Laura's night table registered 2:58 a.m. when she emerged from sleep to hear smothered groans emanating from Enzo's suite. Sitting up and switching on her bedside lamp, she listened. After several moments of silence, she heard them again, and threw back the covers. Not bothering to snatch up her robe or thrust her feet into her satin mules, she hurried on bare feet down the hallway in her charmeuse nightgown.

His door was shut, as she'd expected. "Enzo? Are you all right?" she called, lightly rapping her knuckles against its gilded, paneled face.

He didn't answer. A moment later, he groaned again. What if he's sick? she thought. Reluctant to invade his privacy, she tried the door. To her relief, it wasn't locked. Dark except for a shaft of moonlight that fell across the foot of his bed, the room was a cavern of shadows and looming shapes. Gradually her eyes adjusted. Thrashing and mumbling in his sleep, the brother-in-law she'd come to love more profoundly with each passing day was in the grip of a powerful nightmare.

Half-afraid he'd strike out at her without realizing it, she approached and shook him by the shoulders. "Enzo!" she cried. "Wake up!"

Flinching as if she'd struck him, he opened his eyes. And then blinked in confusion. "Laura? Sweetheart...what are you doing here?" he asked.

The endearment wasn't lost on her, though she didn't stop to revel in it. "You were having a bad dream."

In a rush, the scenario his unconscious had produced came back to him, causing a ripple of nausea in his gut. It was always the same. A fight, seemingly in the Villa Voglia stable. The realization that he'd stabbed and killed someone. Stretching his hands out in front of him, and discovering to his horror that they were covered with blood. Incredibly, though he was shaken to the core, he no longer had his headache.

Operating strictly on instinct, Laura got into bed with him. To her relief, though he slept in the buff, he didn't protest. Instead, he simply let her hold him. For several minutes, they lay quietly together, embracing, with her cheek against his hair. Their legs—his hard and furred with dark body hair, hers smooth beneath her gown's supple fabric—were tangled together. With one hand, she stroked the powerful muscles of his shoulders, soothing him as if he were a baby.

Finally she decided he was calm enough. "Tell me about your dream," she said.

"You don't want to hear."

"I asked, didn't I?"

There was a long silence in which she sensed strong resistance emanating from him. His muscles were tensing up again. "It's always the same," he said reluctantly. "I've dreamed it for years."

"Maybe if you talk about it, you won't have to dream it again."

She could feel him mulling over whether to trust her with an aspect of himself he considered less than flattering. Ultimately he did. "There's a fight," he revealed, in an off-hand tone he might have used to comment on the weather. "I have blood on my hands. It's clear to me that I've killed someone."

"Oh, Enzo! How terrible!" She held him a little tighter. "But you know, don't you . . . dreams aren't something you have to take responsibility for. . . . From what I've read, they're more like a message from your unconscious . . . a wake-up call about something you need to pay attention to."

"Laura, believe me, I've thought about it. The message of my dream is clear. I can't be trusted. I have a terrible temper."

I don't believe that! she wanted to shout. Yet she knew from experience that his emotions ran deep. Unwilling to superimpose her thoughts on his, she waited.

"The dream is about my temper," he went on after a moment. "I view it as a warning. When I was seventeen or so, it was damn near uncontrollable. I took a horsewhip to Stefano once, when I caught him forcing his attentions on one of the maids. He still wears the scar, in case you haven't noticed."

Laura's heart was aching for him. "I *have* noticed," she said. "Stefano deserved what you did. As for the accident with your former fiancée..."

"She was out of her head...trying to kill us both. But I drove her to it. I never really loved her. Our betrothal was largely arranged by my father for business purposes. But I was insanely jealous of her. I found out Stefano had seduced her after we were engaged, and I chose to confront her with my knowledge on the way to our wedding rehearsal. I called her every filthy name in the book... threatened to denounce her in front of the priest and all our relatives...."

To Laura, the outbursts of temper he'd described were mostly justified. They also reflected the actions of a much younger man. From what she could tell, at the age of thirty-eight, Enzo was settled, the responsible chief operating officer of an important company. She doubted he'd vent his anger in the way he had when he was seventeen, or even thirty.

"Whatever happened in the past is past," she told him in no uncertain terms. "You're not the same person you were then. I don't think..."

Sighing, he dismissed her argument as having no validity. "My temper's like a beast inside me," he said, "waiting to gain ascendancy. When my black moods descend, I can feel it straining at the leash. Somehow, Stefano's always connected with it. But I can't be sure I wouldn't turn it loose on someone else. That's part of the reason I never got engaged again, or let myself get serious about anyone. Don't think for a moment that I don't have a normal man's desires...."

His supposed mistress in the Lake District the farthest thing from her thoughts, she kissed his cheek. "*Caro*, I never thought that," she whispered.

Abruptly, they were mouth to mouth. His kiss was lingering and deep, a voyage to her very soul. Yet for that night, at least, she knew, he wouldn't avail himself of her body's comfort.

A moment later, he drew her head against his shoulder, confirming her speculation. "Do me a favor," he said softly. "Don't tell anyone what I told you about the nightmares. Stefano would taunt me. And I don't want to lose my grandmother's respect."

Though it was unorthodox, to say the least, they finished the night together in Enzo's bed. Her head swimming with the currents of Enzo's revelations and his surprising vulnerability, Laura finally went back to sleep around 4:00 a.m. She awakened three hours later to hear the shower running. I suppose I'd better shower and get dressed myself, she thought, reluctantly abandoning the rumpled nest they'd shared. I don't want to push Enzo into intimacy if he isn't ready for it. We have a lot to think about.

Breakfast at his dining-room table was fairly spartan—toast, fruit and coffee served by Claudio Chin, Enzo's Chinese-Italian houseman. It was just as well. Conversing in monosyllables, neither of them had a hearty appetite. Sim-

ilarly, in the car on their way back to the Villa Voglia, they
didn't talk very much.

Yet, amazingly, their silences weren't awkward ones.
Laura could sense a new, more comfortable closeness
springing up. He'd revealed the worst, and she hadn't turned
away from him. On the contrary, she'd offered comfort and
affection.

The only thing she hadn't done was tell him about her
dizzy spells. Or her notion that they might be connected by
a shared past-life experience—one that influenced their
present well-being, and boded ill. If she had, she feared, it
might have driven him away again. Too many problems already separated them.

As they turned into the villa drive, Enzo slowed their forward thrust. "Give me a little time to think about what we
said to each other last night," he asked, reaching across the
gearshift to rest one hand on her knee. "We'll talk soon.
Before we do, I've got to get a few things straight in my
head."

Spoken like a promise, his remarks were vague enough to
be tantalizing without offering a great deal of comfort. I'm
not sure about you, Laura told him silently. But I'm in love
like I've never been before. I wish I knew what I wanted to
do about it. The possibilities boggled her imagination.

Anna and Paolo were picking flowers in the garden as
they drew up to the steps of the villa. Spotting her, Paolo
hurled himself forward. He could barely wait until she got
out of the car before flinging his arms around her neck.

"Mommy, Mommy..." he complained. "'Nardo was here
while you were gone. He was mean to me."

Laura's gaze sought Anna's. "What happened?" she said.

Enzo's mother shook her head regretfully. "Cristina
stopped by for a few hours yesterday afternoon," she said.
"While she was here, 'Nardo caught a snake in the woods.

Thank heaven it wasn't poisonous. He put it in Paolo's bed."

Laura was horrified. "I won't have him preying on my little boy!" she exclaimed.

The older woman patted her arm. "You needn't worry. His riding privileges have been revoked for the winter. And I made him apologize. I don't think he'll try anything like that again."

Furious at Cristina, whom she suspected had secretly approved of her son's misbehavior, Laura hugged Paolo close. Meanwhile, Enzo was giving the boy a thoughtful look. "When 'Nardo put the snake in your bed, whom did you run to?" he asked.

Paolo stared at his uncle with wide eyes. "Anna," he whispered.

Enzo nodded, satisfied. "You mean *Grandmother*."

Chapter Nine

They'd become a family. That's what Enzo meant when he instructed Paolo to call Anna 'Grandmother,' Laura thought several mornings later, peeling an orange as she waited for her son to finish his soft-boiled egg and toast. We're not among strangers anymore. The Villa Voglia has become a kind of second home to us.

In addition to Laura and Paolo, Anna was seated at the round, lace-covered table in the breakfast room, quietly reading that morning's edition of *La Stampa*, the Turin paper. Enzo had gone into the city for the day, but was expected at nightfall. Though Emilia had joined them briefly for coffee, she'd retreated to her room. As usual, Stefano was off working somewhere on the estate. Except for Margherita and Gemma, who were busy with their daily tasks, they had the villa's first floor to themselves.

I wonder what Anna would say if I told her the truth about my dizzy spells, Laura thought, studying her mother-in-law's gentle, once pretty face over the blue-and-white coffee cups. What if I told her I instinctively recognized the villa when Enzo brought me here that first afternoon? Would she think me crazy if I broached the subject of reincarnation with her?

Setting her paper aside, Anna glanced up, as if she'd sensed that Laura had something on her mind. "What is it, dear child?" she asked. "Since you came down to breakfast this morning, I've felt the wheels turning."

Now that she'd been given an opportunity to speak, Laura hesitated.

"You can tell me," the older woman added. "I'm not terribly important in the scheme of things around here. But I know how to keep a confidence."

Try though she would, Laura couldn't detect a trace of irony in Anna's tone. Instead of inviting sympathy, she seemed simply to be stating the truth as she saw it.

By now, Paolo had finished his breakfast. "May I go outside to play with my airplane by the fountain, Mommy?" he asked.

"Yes, you may, darling. But don't fall in the water," Laura cautioned. She waited a moment for him to leave the room before turning back to her mother-in-law. "The fact is," she revealed, "I was wondering if you believed in past lives. I didn't, until recently. Now I wonder. Some fairly strange things have been happening. I feel as if I'm going to burst if I can't discuss them with someone."

Her mother-in-law's gray-green eyes lit with interest. "*What* things, Laura?" she asked.

Slowly, making sure Margherita and Gemma remained out of earshot, Laura outlined her experience at the Art Institute and went on to describe subsequent occurrences of the same phenomenon in the villa gardens and the guest room Emilia had assigned to her.

Instead of voicing skepticism or countering with a comparable experience of her own, Anna listened with an in-

tent expression. Her interest appeared to quicken when
Laura described her sense of familiarity on first arriving at
the villa, and her feeling of déjà vu whenever she went near
the stable. However, she didn't know anything more about
it, or the Uccellis, than Enzo had already revealed.

"So...what do you think?" Laura asked finally, running out of steam. "Are there such things as past lives?
Corridors that stretch between past and present, allowing us
to bridge the gap between them? Or have I been letting my
imagination run away with me? If so, I don't understand
what's prompted me to behave that way. I may be creative
professionally, but I've always considered myself a fairly
sensible person."

Anna regarded her thoughtfully for a moment. "I'm
afraid I don't have any hard and fast answers for you," she
said. "But I must admit. I've done some thinking along the
lines you have. And I've concluded that what you're suggesting isn't so farfetched. In fact..." She paused. "Though
Enzo and Emilia probably wouldn't approve, I've paid several visits to a psychic. I've never taken part in one myself.
But I understand she does past-life regressions."

The two women looked at each other. Unspoken thoughts
danced like moths in the air between them.

"Her name's Alice Kidwell," Anna added. "She's Brit-
ish...an expatriate who works out of her San Remo apartment. We could visit her today, if you like."

For Laura, the opportunity to consult a self-styled expert, whatever her qualifications, was too tempting to miss.
"I'm not sure I'd want to be regressed," she cautioned. "It
might be too much like the spells I've experienced for comfort. But I wouldn't mind talking to her...getting her
opinion, at least."

Anna nodded. "That sounds reasonable. Why don't you
wait until you meet her, and then decide?"

"What about Paolo? I don't want to take him along on that kind of jaunt."

"Gemma can watch him."

A small silence followed.

"All right," Laura said.

Anna's eyes sparkled with anticipation. "My psychic friend rarely overbooks. I'll phone and see if I can get us an appointment."

As it turned out, Alice Kidwell had an hour free that afternoon. "I'll tell Gemma," Anna volunteered. "Why don't you run upstairs and get the sketchpad with the nobleman's portrait? I'd really like to see it. And it might prove helpful."

The trip to San Remo in Anna's modest Fiat—the only car not made at Rossi Motorworks that Laura had seen a family member drive during her visit—was an agreeable one. Though by now it was midautumn, they were headed toward the Mediterranean, and the weather was balmy. Their route across the mountains to the sea took them through Taggia, a town of echoing alleyways and cicadas droning in the underbrush. The coast—famed for jewel thieves, gambling and movie stars—took Laura's breath away. Blue dissolved into blue where the sea met the sky. Boats dotted a succession of harbors. Flowers of every description spilled over masonry walls and filled an array of flowerpots.

As they rounded a bend in the road, the twin headlands and yacht basin of San Remo came into view. Alice Kidwell's residence and place of business was situated on the Corso Nuvoloni, a precipitous, palm-fringed thoroughfare lined with apartment buildings, villas and medium-sized hotels. Seemingly uninfluenced by its surroundings, her fourth-floor flat was chintzy, crammed with bric-a-brac, and very English. As her secretary ushered them into a dimly lit study, Laura glimpsed a balcony overlooking the port.

There's so much of Italy I haven't seen, she thought, trying to assuage her nervousness.

To her relief, Mrs. Kidwell didn't keep them waiting long. "So, Signora Rossi, it's good to see you," the plump, fiftyish psychic said cheerfully as she entered and took a chair across from them behind a small square table. "This must be your daughter-in-law, Laura. A pleasure meeting you, dear. How may I be of service?"

Laura and Anna exchanged a look.

"Would you like me to step into the next room?" Anna offered. "I won't mind, if you'd feel more comfortable."

Reaching between their chairs, Laura caught hold of her hand. "No. Stay. I want you to."

A bit hesitantly at first, she repeated what she'd told Anna at the breakfast table and opened her sketchpad to show Alice Kidwell her sketch of the Renaissance nobleman. In describing her reaction the first time she'd seen his painted image, she forgot to mention Cardinal Uccelli's portrait. Deferential as she always was when someone else was speaking, Anna didn't supply the missing information.

"Every time I've turned around recently, I've stubbed my toe on the past," Laura concluded. "I want to know if contact across the centuries is possible . . . whether the concept of reincarnation is a valid one."

The psychic studied her for a moment. "Yes on both counts," she said, "if my personal belief counts for anything. I get the distinct impression a specific incident has carried over in your case. Have you considered being regressed?"

On the way to San Remo, Laura had decided not to chance it. She hadn't felt comfortable with the idea of abdicating that much control. Now she was tempted to reconsider. If she could determine the cause of her dizzy spells—unearth the link she sensed connected them and her powerful attraction to Enzo—whatever trauma resulted might be worth it.

"I'm not wild about the idea," she admitted. "I might be willing to give it a try, though. What could I expect?"

The psychic gave her hand a reassuring pat. "Nothing so dreadful, as you won't be going back to the past in body, just reliving it in soul memory. We'll begin by relaxing you . . . and, in the process, inducing a light trance. When you're sufficiently tranquil and open to suggestion, I'll ask you to choose a year . . . any year in history. I can't emphasize strongly enough that you should go with the first one that crosses your mind.

"Next, I'll ask you to envision a scene. When one presents itself, it's likely you'll identify with one of the participants. You may feel as if you were once that person. It may be an everyday scene. Perhaps even a boring one. Whatever the case, allow it to play out without attempting to guide it. It's possible you'll merge in imagination with the person you've identified with, feel as if the scene is actually happening. If you do, you'll be able to think his or her thoughts, regain lost emotion. . . ."

Laura stared. "*His or her?* You mean . . ."

The psychic gave her an amused smile. "Most reincarnationists believe that we've each been men and women at different times in our soul's history," she said. "Don't worry about it if you identify with a member of the opposite sex. Just take whatever comes up. The same thing goes for what's happening in the scene. Allow its details to elaborate, no matter how mundane or trivial they might seem."

Laura was silent a moment, considering. "And if the emotions get to be too much for me?" she asked.

"I'll bring you back. At once. I guarantee it. You'll be perfectly safe in my hands."

Glancing at Anna, who watched her closely for her reaction but didn't offer advice, Laura mulled over the situation for a moment. She was still reluctant to go ahead. Yet she felt the opportunity was too good to miss.

"All right," she said at last. "I may as well give it a whirl."

Mrs. Kidwell nodded. "Good!" she said in her cheery way, waving Laura to a chintz-covered couch. "If you'll be so kind as to take off your shoes, Laura... Lie down and shut your eyes... we'll get started right away."

The down-filled throw pillows on Mrs. Kidwell's chaise accommodated themselves perfectly to the back of Laura's neck. To her surprise, as the expatriate Englishwoman began, with directions issued in a soothing monotone, to relax her toes, feet and ankles, the tension she'd felt over being regressed to a past life began to seep from her body. In its place, a state of comfort, trust and relaxed expectancy grew. By the time the psychic asked her to state what year it was, she felt light, almost boneless, and more than willing to cooperate.

A date leapt obligingly into her head. "It's 1520," she whispered.

"What's happening?"

"I'm not sure...."

As Laura watched in her mind's eye, a young girl of about sixteen, in a floor-length gown, approached the open door to a high-ceilinged room, then hesitated, as if slightly fearful. Inside, two men were arguing. They appeared to be mirror images of each other. One wore black, the other scarlet. "I'm telling you for the last time...your household expenses are disgracefully high. I can't afford to give you anything further from the estate's earnings," the one in the black velvet doublet decreed.

"You can sell the land our maternal grandfather left you," the other replied.

"That's out of the question. I've a wife, now, to maintain. I hope to beget children. You're a man of God, aren't you? Drink less wine. Keep fewer women. Live within your portion of our inheritance."

The man in scarlet shot back a lewd response. Incredibly, it alluded to the young girl. She gasped to hear herself called a "pretty filly to ride." Her face flamed as the man in scarlet added, "Too bad you'll turn her into a brood mare, fat and lazy. I've half a mind to sample her favors first."

His dark eyes murderous, the man in black seized his twin by the throat. They began to struggle as the young girl covered her mouth and held her breath.

"What is it?" Mrs. Kidwell asked.

Laura shook her head. The scene had dissolved to be replaced by another, one that she instinctively recognized had occurred at a somewhat later date. It was evening. Dusk, in actuality. Somewhere a raven croaked and then fell silent. The young girl was walking down a soft dirt path toward . . . toward . . . *the stable*.

Her favorite mare had recently foaled.

"No!" Laura blurted. "It's not safe! What he'll do will kill you. *He's* waiting for you there!"

As good as her word, Mrs. Kidwell began easing Laura from her trance at the first sign of genuine distress. A moment or two later, Laura was sitting up and flexing her fingers. They felt stiff and tingly, as if their blood supply had been constricted and they'd fallen asleep. In general, she felt a little light-headed. Details of the supposed past-life scenes she'd conjured up were fading fast.

Perhaps to fix them in her mind, the psychic questioned her. She was able to describe the warring brothers, her feelings on the path to what she believed was the Villa Voglia stable. But she couldn't name the man she'd felt was waiting for her counterpart there. Or be specific about the danger she'd warned against.

During the remainder of their time with her, Mrs. Kidwell commented in some detail on the visions Laura had seen during her dizzy spells. In her opinion, the scenes were related to an event of some magnitude in a previous life, or a crucial moment in the villa's history. Perhaps both.

Laura found it difficult to accept the latter suggestion. "How can that be, when I had my first visions in Chicago?" she asked.

Mrs. Kidwell shrugged. "I don't see any conflict. Whether or not you were linked with the Villa Voglia in an earlier incarnation, you may be extraordinarily psychic. Yes, I know . . . you haven't had any evidence of that. It's possible your powers haven't previously been tested."

As they said goodbye a short time later, the expatriate Englishwoman added a warning. "Tread carefully, dear," she advised, almost as an afterthought. "The events of the next few weeks will be pivotal."

When Enzo returned to the villa, Laura didn't confide the day's adventure to him. In part, that was because a new wrinkle in the settlement of Umberto's estate had claimed everyone's attention. Because of a family emergency that would put him in London on the day Umberto's will had been scheduled to be read, Dino Lucchanti had asked them to move up the date. In fact, he wanted them to meet him in his office the following morning.

I'm not sure I'm ready for the kind of confrontation with Cristina this is going to entail, Laura thought as Enzo informed his grandmother that Sofia had agreed to drive up from San Remo for the session. "With everyone else readily available, I didn't see any reason to postpone the meeting until Dino's return," he said. "If there's to be unpleasantness over the will, we may as well get it over with."

In the morning, Stefano left early. In response to a question from Emilia, he murmured something about "business to transact" before reporting to the attorney's office. Cristina and Vittorio had been back in the city for several days. That left Laura, Anna and Emilia to drive with Enzo in the Rossi matriarch's luxurious black sedan.

Before getting behind the wheel, Enzo took Laura aside and whispered that he hoped to speak with her privately when they returned.

"What about?" she asked, her rose-printed silk skirt blowing about her legs as they stood with their backs to the others.

"The matter we discussed in Turin, along with several others." He lightly stroked the inside of her wrist, causing her pulse to quicken, as Anna and Emilia waited in the car for them. "I couldn't sleep last night, and, as a result, I did a lot of thinking," he added. "I'm anxious to talk with you."

On their drive into the city, Laura couldn't stop speculating about his intent. Would he announce that he wanted to make love to her despite his scruples? Or did he contemplate a far more serious step . . . one she wasn't quite ready to think about?

As luck would have it, they arrived at the iron-grilled entrance to the attorney's office at the precise moment Cristina and Vittorio did. The slender brunette's features were frozen in a stiff, angry expression. She refused to make eye contact.

"After you," Enzo said, giving way. By rights, with Emilia on his arm, he should have taken precedence.

Uncomfortable as she seemed to be with this breach of family etiquette, Cristina was clearly too irate to take advantage of it. As Dino Lucchanti's secretary ushered them into his inner sanctum, the tension in the air was suffocating.

Stefano arrived a moment later. They were ready to start. In an obvious effort to put a friendly veneer on the situation, the lawyer shook hands with everyone. A row of chairs had been arranged in a semicircle facing his desk. Laura chose a seat between Anna and Enzo. When everyone was settled, their host opened the folder that lay on the desktop in front of him and cleared his throat.

Written in Italian legalese, which Laura found relatively easy to follow, thanks to her recent immersion in the language, the new will Umberto had asked the lawyer to draw up while his unsuspecting family was working in the fields was the essence of simplicity. Enzo got forty percent of Rossi Motorworks, with the remainder of the privately held company's stock to be divided equally among Sofia, Cristina and Paolo, who—the lawyer pointed out—had been named in place of his deceased father. Both grandsons got gifts of bank stock Umberto had owned, to be managed in trust by their parents until their twenty-first birthdays, plus lump sums earmarked for their education.

Cristina's expression was thunderous. To her credit, she didn't interrupt as the attorney enumerated the other bequests, including cash, additional bank stock and extensive real estate to Emilia and Anna. Stefano got a generous sum in cash, some rental property in Turin and a small local farm, separate from the Villa Voglia holdings, which produced excellent grapes. He was also granted lifelong residence at the Rossi country home, though its deed would pass into Enzo's hands. Perhaps with an eye to emphasizing his familial tie to the others, though he didn't share in the Rossi Motorworks stock, the legacy didn't oblige him to continue as estate manager in order to exercise the privilege.

At last even the bequests to charitable foundations had been read. "That's everything," Dino Lucchanti concluded, glancing at each of them in turn. "My secretary has made copies of the will for you. Go over it at your leisure, bearing in mind that objections must be filed within thirty days. If none are lodged, Signor Rossi's assets will be disbursed as soon as the deadline has passed. Are there any questions?''

No one seemed surprised when Cristina raised a slender, beringed hand. ''You may as well know, Signor Lucchanti,'' she said, her tone as taut as piano wire. ''There will be *two* objections. My husband, Vittorio Marchese, and I plan to protest the inclusion of my late brother Guy's son, Paolo. Until recently, my father had nothing to do with the boy. They'd never even met. Then Enzo brought him here. We believe his mother, Laura Rossi, put undue pressure on my father, badgering him to change his will in Paolo's favor at a time when his thinking wasn't clear.''

Laura gasped in outrage. ''That's not true!'' she exclaimed. ''I'd *never* do such a thing!''

Both Emilia and Anna glared at Cristina in disapproval. Tightly gripping Laura's hand, Enzo urged restraint. ''Not now,'' he whispered.

Cristina went on as if Laura hadn't spoken. ''My half brother, Stefano, can tell you about the other objection, since he's the one who'll be making it,'' she said carelessly.

Several blinks of astonishment greeted the news, including one from Emilia. All eyes turned to the family outsider, who, as befitted his status, was seated a little apart, by the windows.

''I hadn't planned to mention it today, but since Cristina has forced the issue, I may as well,'' he revealed with a shrug. ''As I told her earlier this morning, I have as much claim on Rossi Motorworks as Umberto's other children. Double that of Paolo, as I'm a direct descendant. Since I didn't receive an equal share of the company stock, as they did, I plan to litigate.''

A muscle twitched along Enzo's jaw as he stared at his half brother in consternation. While Cristina's mischief is aimed at disinheriting Paolo, Stefano's has *me* as its primary target, he realized. He plans to retaliate for every fight we've ever had, every imagined slight he's suffered since we were teenagers.

Swift calculation confirmed the unhappy fact that, if somehow he could get both half-sisters to support him after successfully challenging the will, Stefano could lord it over him in the area of influence he'd considered most inviolate—the company his father had groomed him to lead one day. He'd taken steps in that direction already, unless Enzo missed his guess. Cristina's never had any use for him, he thought. Yet they've talked privately about this. Whatever agreement she reaches with him will be out of spite.

If Stefano won and Cristina lost, on the other hand, Enzo stood a good chance of retaining control. He'd have to vote Paolo's stock to do it, though. And that meant getting Laura's consent. She'll come to that conclusion on her own, he realized. He couldn't help but wonder how she'd integrate the knowledge when he told her how he felt. Would she believe his intentions were sincere? Or think his motives were mercenary? Whatever the case, her planned departure was just a few days hence. He couldn't afford to postpone having things out with her.

Sofia had been unmoved, almost placid, throughout the reading. She already received a sizable alimony payment each month from her ex-husband, Enzo knew. For her, the inheritance from their father was pure gravy. He wasn't too surprised when, murmuring something about a few days' shopping in Milan, she was the first family member to depart.

A moment later, Anna excused herself to use the rest room.

Clearly uncomfortable with Emilia's displeasure, though she gave no sign of abandoning her adversarial position, Cristina engaged her grandmother in hushed, earnest conversation. Vittorio stood at her side, awkwardly flexing his long, pale fingers. With an apologetic glance at Laura, Enzo joined them, in self-defense.

Feeling herself to be the ultimate Rossi outsider, and still seething over Cristina's accusation that she'd taken advantage of a dying man, Laura stepped into the hall to wait. She couldn't help wincing when Stefano followed her from the lawyer's office.

About to brush past her with a nod, he hesitated. "Whatever your opinion of me and my plan to challenge Enzo for control of the company," he said, "I like you, Laura. I wouldn't want to see you hurt. Yet that's just what I'm afraid will happen if Emilia gets her way...."

Letting the statement dangle like a loose thread, he invited her to unravel it.

"I don't know what you're talking about," she said.

"No... I don't suppose you do." Leaning a little closer, though there was no one in the hall to overhear them, Stefano appeared to gaze at her with sympathy. "Ever the pragmatist, my grandmother wants Enzo to marry you so your little boy will remain in Italy," he disclosed. "I overheard them speaking about it some time ago. Now that the will's been read and my plans noted, he'll have reasons of his own for honoring her wishes. In my opinion, you deserve better—a man who'll love you for yourself."

Inevitably, conversation was somewhat stilted in the yellow-silk-paneled dining room at the Palazzo Rossi, where Enzo, Laura, Emilia and Anna retired for lunch. Though Cristina's and Stefano's plans to contest the will were almost certainly uppermost in everyone's minds, the topic wasn't even mentioned. For one thing, Emilia's manner forbade it. An aristocrat of the old school, she made it clear by her own failure to speak of it that she wouldn't tolerate any discussion of the wrangle they'd just witnessed.

Pushing her food about on her plate while eating very little, Laura thought about what Stefano had said. Surely he was lying when he said Emilia wants Enzo to marry me just to keep Paolo in Italy, she thought. I know family's first and foremost to her. I just can't believe she'd be that Machiavellian. As the Rossi matriarch's sedan ate up the miles of woods, rolling hills and meandering tributaries to the Po that separated the family's city and country residences a short time later, she was deep in thought.

Gemma had put Paolo down for his nap by the time they arrived. Declaring that they, too, needed rest, Emilia and Anna retreated to their rooms. Upset by the day's events and keenly aware that her days in Italy were almost at an end, Laura started to follow them. With nothing better to do, she might as well organize their belongings for the return trip. Her heady stream of romantic speculation over what Enzo had meant by his remarks that morning had long since narrowed to a trickle of misgivings and uncertainty.

Emerging from his study, where he'd gone to collect his phone messages, Enzo caught up with her at the landing. "Come...walk with me in the garden," he demanded, taking possession of her hand. "We were going to talk this afternoon, remember?"

A shiver of anticipation knifed through her, despite her reservations. *This is it,* a prescient little voice whispered inside her head. *The moment of truth. Your life has reached a watershed.*

Stefano's wrong, she tried to convince herself as Enzo let her back down the stairs. He won't ask you to marry him just because that's what Emilia wants. He'd never use you as a pawn to please her, or to retain control of Rossi Motorworks.

Yet as they went outside to stroll past the rhythmically splashing fountain, down a neatly raked gravel path, to a rise that overlooked the estate's vista of vine-clad hills, she had the unsteady sensation of a woman flirting with the edge of a precipice. From their first goodbye, when his handshake at her front door had penetrated her defenses more deeply than a kiss could have, she'd felt herself tumbling into a profound harmony with him.

He's your destiny, she thought as his fingers curled about hers. And that's not a completely positive thing. Stefano's warning aside, she sensed a potent element of danger in any personal relationship they might share. Yet, to save herself—to reach the terra firma of her life in Chicago again—she'd have to go against her heart.

Pausing beneath an arbor that had been positioned to frame the view, Enzo glanced back toward the house. He'd seen Stefano's Imperata roadster parked near the stable on their arrival, so presumably his half brother was somewhere about the property. Though no movement was visible at the windows, he had the strong feeling his half brother was watching them. Go ahead! he thought angrily. If Laura feels as I do, your jealousy can't hurt us.

His gaze softened a moment later as he rested it on her upturned face. I thought my life was set in a pattern of overwork and loneliness, he acknowledged silently, putting his arms about her waist. Then *you* came along. I began to dream of incredible possibilities. Just the way your skirt's soft folds betray the shape of your thighs makes me ache to lie between them, to create with you a delight so deep we'll never again be completely separate.

"When we talked at my apartment that night, after dancing at the African Club, I wanted to tell you how I feel about you," he confessed, lightly kissing the tip of her nose. "I wouldn't let myself. I thought that, because of my moodiness and nightmares, the terrible temper Stefano swears I possess, I didn't have the right. In light of what losing you would mean, I've reconsidered...."

Is he doing this because Emilia wants him to? Laura wondered, hating herself for the thought. Or did Stefano's challenge to his authority at Rossi Motorworks inspire it? She didn't want to mistrust Enzo. At the same time, she had the feeling he'd do almost anything to avoid letting his half brother take advantage of him.

Abruptly, though no dizzy spell announced its presence, she felt the past hovering close. Words spoken by an unseen man as she snipped flowers for a centerpiece in the villa's garden resurfaced in her thoughts.

Marry me, Rafaella...

Had it all happened before, give or take a few hundred years? Or had the sixteenth-century convergence she sensed taken place near the spot where they were standing now united two completely different persons?

"Enzo, I don't think..." she began worriedly.

He continued to speak as if no remonstrance had passed her lips. "I'm asking you to marry me, Laura. I realize that, despite the material advantages I can offer you, I may not be the best of marriage prospects. Yet surely you realize... I'd cherish you, do my best to make the kind of life you and Paolo deserve."

Her feet in quicksand, her heart hammering in her throat, Laura tried not to lose sight of what was actually happening. He hasn't mentioned love, she thought fiercely. Or eased my mind about Stefano's accusations. She had a powerful feeling that, if she and Enzo dared to reach for happiness together, disaster would result.

His eyes glittering with pent-up emotion, he waited for her to speak.

"I can't believe you're serious," she said at last, unearthing whatever negative arguments she could. "We've known each other such a short time. Our worlds are so very different...."

Having conquered his scruples, Enzo had no intention of letting her sink his proposal without a fight. "Guy was a product of this environment," he reminded. "Yet you married him. You claim to have been very happy. He and I aren't... *weren't*... so very different."

Struggling awake from one of his nightmares or moodily contemplating Stefano's latest challenge, Enzo was as different from Guy as night from morning, shadow from sunbeams streaming in a window. Whereas Guy had been carefree, a charming young man who'd cut his losses and kept his commitments light, except for her, Enzo was deeply attached to Rossi Motorworks and the Villa Voglia. He brooded over mistakes—felt the full weight of his responsibilities.

Yet she'd seen his lighter side. And felt drawn to it. Away from the villa and his half brother's jealousy, she'd found him sunny-natured and affectionate. The resonance of his personality had drawn her like a magnet.

In his dreams, the man has blood on his hands, she reminded herself. It isn't the best of portents.

"Aren't you going to give me an answer?" he asked, lightly tracing the shape of her mouth. "I love you so much."

The words she'd been longing to hear twisted in her heart. Could she believe them? Was Enzo the intense, brooding but essentially trustworthy man she wanted him to be—one with a largely untapped capacity for laughter and affection? Or merely a pragmatist given to pretty speeches? The mercenary businessman with an ungovernable temper Stefano had painted?

The warmth of his nearness was drugging her senses. "What about my business?" she asked. "If we married, I'd have to give up living in the States."

"Such practicality, at a moment like this!" Gently teasing, he leaned his forehead against hers. "Couldn't you operate it from two continents, *cara?* Other designers and executives do. All you could possibly want in terms of materials and inspiration is nearby—the fabric houses of Como and Turin, Milanese couture. Your partner could handle the marketing and business end of your operation in New York. You could travel there whenever you wanted."

Obviously he'd cared enough about her professional concerns to think them through. And he was right, in essence. Commuting *would* work, if she gave it her best. An Italian base would give Rossi Originals international prominence.

Unbidden, a favorite aphorism of Guy's drifted through her head. Life hands us trouble, he'd said. It's up to us to make our own happiness.

Jettisoning her fears and the suspicions Stefano had planted outside the lawyer's office would be like stepping off a cliff with no one to catch her. So would agreeing to make her home in Italy, with only periodic trips to the States. Yet it was exactly what she wanted. She *loved* Enzo. During the brief span of her visit, the thought of life without him had become as bleak as winter's grip on Lake Michigan.

Sighing, she allowed her resistance to melt. What would be, would be. She'd take the consequences.

"All right, Enzo," she whispered, stunning him with the suddenness of her capitulation. "I love you, too. I'll marry you, if that's what you want."

Chapter Ten

They announced their engagement the following morning at the breakfast table. Deliriously happy, yet uneasy at taking such an irrevocable step with so many unanswered questions buzzing in her head, Laura quivered like a bowstring at the erotic awareness that flowed from Enzo's fingers to hers as he outlined their plans to Anna and his grandmother. Whatever his motives for proposing marriage, she knew he wanted her as much as she wanted him. The previous afternoon, when he'd enfolded her in the garden, crushing her mouth with his as if it were made of ripe red raspberries, she'd felt the hard column of his desire pressing against her leg. Her response had been immediate. Aroused in her most feminine recesses, she'd ached to feel him there.

The same thing had happened later, when he'd kissed her good-night outside her door. If it hadn't been for Paolo, asleep in the next room, and Emilia with her reading lamp still lit just down the hall, she knew he'd have suggested sharing her bed. And she'd have let him. It's fortunate for our peace of mind, she thought, that we're to be married right away. Even now, as she stood demurely at Enzo's side, the thought of his hairy, muscular body nestled between her sheets was a powerful aphrodisiac.

Lingering over an unaccustomed second cup of coffee, Stefano watched them with impassive interest. She only hoped he couldn't guess what she was thinking.

"If you have no objection, Grandmother," Enzo was saying, "we'll hold the wedding day after tomorrow, in the little chapel, with just a few family members present. It's too soon after Father's funeral to do anything else."

Hooded and usually difficult to read, Emilia's dark eyes glittered with satisfaction. Yet her patrician calm remained firmly in place. "I don't mind admitting I'm pleased the two of you found each other," she said, a bit tartly. "However, I fail to understand the rush. Doesn't the church impose a waiting period?"

"Father Tomasi has agreed to waive the banns. I've taken the liberty of asking him to officiate. Yes, I know. Your brother, Cardinal Sforza, usually does the honors. But he's in Brussels at the moment. And we don't want to wait."

"I think the whole thing's perfectly wonderful. In my opinion, you *shouldn't* wait a bit." Pushing back her chair, Anna rose and came around the table to embrace them both. "My blessings on you, son," she added to Enzo. "Just when I'd given up hope you'd ever marry, you've chosen well. As for you, Laura, you'll be doubly my daughter-in-law. I can't think of a nicer situation."

For once, the turned-down corners of Emilia's mouth were complaisant as she watched. "What about you, Stefano?" she prodded with a little lemon-squeeze of irony. "Aren't you going to congratulate your brother?"

"Of course, Grandmother." Dutifully, but with an awkwardness that betrayed his true feelings, Stefano got to his feet. "I wish you both the best," he said, his smile more twisted than Laura could remember seeing it.

The gathering around the breakfast table broke up quickly after that, with Stefano departing to superintend some job or other on the estate, and Enzo phoning an elderly great-aunt on his father's side, who spent most of the year in Rome. The contessa, as he called her, owned a lovely old villa in the Lake District. Though he had to shout a little to make himself understood, she gave her permission readily enough. Enzo and his bride were more than welcome to use the place for their honeymoon.

After giving Laura the news, Enzo conducted a lengthy conference call with his midlevel managers at the factory. As she waited for sunrise to reach Chicago so that she could phone Carol and announce her radical change in plans, Laura tried to compose a telegram to her parents.

She couldn't begin to imagine what they'd think when they received it. She hadn't *met* Enzo when her mother and father had departed on their latest junket. They were still in Nepal, and now she was marrying him. Her father, who was flexible about most things but operated strictly by the book when it came to the welfare of his one and only daughter, would probably be indignant that she hadn't consulted him.

So, Daddy…what would you have me do? she asked him in her imagination. Seek you out by yak, now that you've left the only hotel in your immediate area of the country that has a telephone? There wouldn't be any point. Nothing you could say or do would make me change my mind. The fact that he'd probably try to do just that, or at least urge her to wait, couldn't be allowed to dissuade her. In a way that seemed tied to her glimpses of another time and place, she sensed her marriage to Enzo was meant to be. That's true, she thought, whether it proves our undoing or our salvation.

By carefully calculating the time difference, she managed to reach Carol before the former schoolteacher had left her near-North apartment. "What is it *this* time?" her partner said with a laugh before she could launch into an explanation. "Are you planning to stay in Italy for good?"

The question evoked embarrassed laughter. "Actually, you've pretty much guessed it," Laura confessed. "Enzo and I are getting married on Friday. I don't suppose you could hop on a plane and stand up for us?"

For a moment the line hummed empty as Carol absorbed the unexpected revelation. Then, "You're serious, aren't you?" she asked. "This isn't a test or something, to see if I'm awake."

"I'm serious."

"Well, congratulations! I'm very happy for you. I had a feeling something romantic was going on...just no idea things had gotten to that stage yet!"

Laura made a face at Carol's allusion to their precipitate courtship. "They *have* been moving rather quickly, haven't they?" she admitted with a trace of embarrassment. "What about flying over? With my parents incommunicado somewhere in the wilds of Nepal, you're the only family I've got."

Briefly Carol considered the request. "Sorry, hon," she decided. "I'd better not. Someone's got to mind the store."

Carol's reference to Rossi Originals and, indirectly, to what Laura considered the gross neglect of her duties inundated the latter with guilt. "Enzo claims we can run the company jointly from Italy and New York," she said apologetically. "Do you think that's possible? Because if it isn't..."

"You'll cancel your plans?"

How can I? Laura thought, holding her breath.

"As a matter of fact, I do think it'll work." Clearly having given the matter some thought before being asked, Carol outlined the advantages as she saw them. "The Italian connection will add cachet to our image," she concluded. "Plus, the fabric samples you sent from Turin are wonderful. So are your Renaissance designs. Instead of turning out to be a drawback, the changes you're making in your life may be just what we've needed to push us into the big league."

Briefly their conversation was put on hold as Enzo reentered the study in search of his reading glasses and Laura put him on the phone to say hello. Lounging against his desk in sandals, pleated tan linen trousers and a white hand-tailored shirt with the sleeves rolled up to reveal his muscular forearms, he looked as relaxed and handsome as an Italian movie star. No doubt he sounds like one to Carol, Laura thought as he chatted easily with her friend. Hearing his accented, perfectly grammatical English from her partner's perspective, Laura found it freshly devastating.

There didn't seem to be much doubt Carol was impressed. "He sounds like a honey!" she said with feeling when Laura had the study and the phone to herself again. "And you're obviously crazy about him. So why do I feel things aren't completely settled between the two of you? Am I imagining things?"

As always, even from a distance of almost five thousand miles, Carol could read her like a book. "Not entirely," Laura admitted. "There's a lot I haven't had a chance to tell you about. For one thing, Enzo's younger sister, Cristina, is suing to cut Paolo out of his grandfather's will. Plus, his half brother, Stefano, is challenging his right to run the family firm. To retain control, Enzo needs Paolo's shares...."

"And you think his motives are grasping?"

"No, I don't!" Aware she might sound as if she were protesting too much, Laura softened her tone. "Not consciously, anyway," she amended. "Enzo says he loves me.

And I believe him. It's just that Stefano predicted he'd ask
me for business reasons a few hours before he proposed.''
Her subtler fears, those based on nightmares and psychic
predictions, seemed too marginal even to discuss.

Carol was silent a moment. She seemed to be considering
what Laura had told her. ''Whatever his aims, the half
brother doesn't impress me as the most disinterested of
parties,'' she remarked. ''If I were you, I'd rely on my in-
stincts. Wait if you have doubts, although I don't suppose
that's advice you're inclined to take.''

As she got into bed the night before her wedding, Laura
was a bundle of nerves. She'd had no additional glimpses of
bygone events. Yet she couldn't help feeling they were just
out of reach. At last she drifted into slumber. For the most
part, her dreams were pleasant. It wasn't until morning that
her subconscious conjured up Cardinal Uccelli, the
churchman in the Turin portrait. In the tableau it created,
he wore a scarlet-faced cloak and rode a horse remarkably
similar to Stefano's. Paolo was perched in the saddle in
front of him.

''Our son will soon be riding on his own, Rafaella,'' he
said, his gaze lecherous and insistent as it drilled into hers.
''Perhaps it's time we made another baby.''

''No,'' Laura cried in a muffled voice as her sleeping body
tossed and turned beneath the bed covers.

Paolo isn't his child! she added in silence, desperately
seeking to distance herself from him. Nor am I his wife.
Princes of the church can't marry anyone.

Her distress and the dream message that had prompted it
had all but faded from memory a short time later, as she sat
up and assessed the eastern sky's first pinkish streaks of
light. As the day unfolded, it proved sunny and mild—utterly glorious for late autumn, to Laura's Chicago-bred
sensibilities.

Lapped by sunlight and leaf shadow as she stood with Enzo, Paolo and Emilia outside the Rossi's private chapel, waiting for the priest to arrive, she managed to convince herself her earlier fears were groundless. *The logic of what I've done is elegantly simple,* she thought. *I love Enzo. Instead of focusing exclusively on work and struggling to raise my son alone, I'm choosing happiness.*

She wasn't prepared for the wave of déjà vu that washed over her. *It's as if we're about to marry for the second time,* she thought, the idea bubbling up from some layer of memory she hadn't known she possessed.

That couldn't be, of course—unless Mrs. Kidwell's suppositions were correct, and each soul lived a multiplicity of lives. Shivering slightly in the warm sunlight, Laura ordered herself not to be fanciful as Enzo slipped one arm around her.

"Are you all right, *cara?*" he asked, concern creasing his forehead. "You look a little pale."

"I'm fine. Honestly." She squeezed his hand to reassure him.

"No second thoughts?"

Their marriage was meant. She knew that much. "None. I'm very happy," she whispered.

To her surprise, though they kept to themselves and appeared as unfriendly as ever where she was concerned, Cristina and Vittorio had taken the trouble to drive down from Turin for the ceremony. Glancing toward the house, she saw Stefano striding toward them across the grass. When he reached the chapel, Stefano didn't shake Enzo's hand. Or unbend sufficiently to wish them the best. Yet he nodded as if to show them deference. Seemingly Rossi blood ties ran deep, despite the rancor that divided one sibling from another.

Approaching and kissing Laura on both cheeks, Anna put a bouquet of freesias into her hands. "A bride must have flowers," she said with her most radiant smile. "Even if she's dressed in black because of a recent funeral. My advice for the two of you is fairly uncomplicated...make each other happy. If you do that, everything else will fall into place."

At last Father Tomasi drove up in a cloud of dust. Together, they moved into the tiny, damp-stained chapel, with its hard, uncomfortable chairs and fragile stained-glass windows. As bride and bridegroom, Laura and Enzo stood in front, facing the priest before the chapel's moldering sixteenth-century altar.

As he began to speak the opening words of the wedding service, the past tugged at her again. We've stood at this altar before and pledged our troth, she thought—innocent of the tragedy that would overtake us.

A moment later, she was banishing the idea from her head. This is the happiest day of my life, she insisted fiercely. I won't think of tragedy. Or ruin it by succumbing to one of my dizzy spells. When they returned from their honeymoon, she'd get to the bottom of things. See a doctor, if necessary. Maybe even a psychiatrist.

Though the service was in Italian, and she felt light-headed in the extreme, she managed to follow almost every word. Once their vows were spoken and the marriage seal was set, Father Tomasi instructed them, they'd be flesh of each other's flesh. Inextricably bound together, until death parted them. What God had joined, no earthly power could put asunder.

Her hands imprisoned in Enzo's, her gaze inextricably linked with his, Laura felt the past that had dogged her footsteps for weeks reassert its claims. This time, she didn't have the strength to resist. We've been married before, she thought unsteadily. In another time. *But in this place.* Something terrible happened to part us. Now we're stitching the rent fabric of our love together.

Somehow, she managed to speak her vows in a clear, committed voice. Enzo did likewise. Yet she could sense his sudden tension, his nervousness. Was he having similar thoughts? Or was he just eager to put the ceremony behind him? When he claimed her for a nuptial kiss, he held her so tightly he almost crushed her ribs.

A veil seemed to lift as they filed outside, accepted hugs and congratulations, sipped several ceremonial glasses of champagne. It had dispersed altogether by the time they left the Villa Voglia in Enzo's Falconetta convertible, headed not for Turin, but for a mountain-fringed lake country so beautiful her new husband had described it as an earthly morsel of paradise.

Whatever disquiet Laura's new husband had felt during the ceremony, it seemed no longer to be a factor. He appeared light and free—the man who'd charmed her in Chicago with his affectionate yet charismatic ways, the air he had of being his own person. As for her bizarre conviction that their marriage paralleled a similar union in the past, she'd decided not to tell him about it yet. Right now, I want to concentrate on loving him, she thought. Being his wife. A courtesan for his pleasure. I want to give him everything.

Before leaving in a shower of rice Anna and Paolo had conspired to throw, they'd changed from the funeral black Emilia had decreed they must wear into comfortable, lightweight clothing. Fluid now in an aqua silk two-piece dress she'd designed herself, with her bouquet of freesias in her lap, Laura turned to the man she'd married and feathered a tender little kiss against his neck.

"I love you, Enzo," she whispered.

"As I love you."

Though his eyes were hidden behind dark sunglasses, Laura could feel their tenderness as he brushed back a lock of her hair and leaned across the gearshift to kiss her mouth. He had to take his eyes off the road to do it. Tongue to tongue and breath to breath, the kiss lengthened. Inevitably, gravel spurted as the Falconetta's racing tires left the pavement.

"Enzo... be careful!" Laura exclaimed.

Laughing, he let go of her and swerved back onto the asphalt. "Don't worry, *cara,*" he teased. "I have every intention of reaching our destination in excellent physical shape."

Northwest of Milan, they took the A9 toward Como. A half hour later, the lake of the same name came breathtakingly into view. Set like a jewel in its narrow, fjord-deep valley between forested hills that had faded to blue in the hazy sunlight, it was so still it almost appeared to be a gentle mirror to the sky. Then a speedboat cut across its surface, its wake pluming white. The ripples that died back flashed lazy glints of silver. Somewhere a church bell rang, echoing and reechoing.

In the more crowded areas of Como's *centro città,* closely spaced buildings lined cobblestone streets, intermittently blocking the lake from view. The traffic was horrendous, probably because the weekend rush was getting under way. Already a horde of tourists jammed the expensive cafés that lined the waterfront.

About a kilometer outside the city, the route leveled off, though it continued to wind around the burly green outcroppings of hills, and they were driving with an unobstructed view of the lake. Ocher and salmon and terra-cotta villas began to appear among the trees along the shore, their variegated barrel-tile roofs liberally dotted with chimneys. Boats of various types were tied up at their water gates, as if to beckon the pleasure-seeker lakeward. White puffs of cloud floated overhead, like sheep grazing on the invisible grass of heaven. The air was incredibly soft and mild—so humid it caressed the skin like velvet. Though it was November, a lush array of camellias was still in bloom.

"Here we are," Enzo announced at last, turning into one of the gravel drives that led downward toward the shore and getting out to open a wrought-iron gate.

Like the Villa Voglia, the elderly contessa's lakeside palazzo had been built during the early Renaissance. Laura stared at its size and symmetrical beauty. "Are we really to have such a place all to ourselves?" she asked.

Enzo threw her an indulgent look. "We are . . . except for a houseboy, a cook and a gardener, who've been warned not to hover too much."

Set at the end of a long reflecting pool between tall, clipped hedges and perfectly spaced cypresses, the villa afforded a gemlike glimpse of blue water through an open-air loggia that cut through its center. Its pink stucco walls had been thinly washed with ivory. Beyond, the mountainous, undulating ridge on the lake's far shore formed a misty blue backdrop.

The houseboy in question materialized to collect their luggage as Enzo parked by the land entrance. "Please . . . hold our bags downstairs," he requested. "When we're ready, we'll ring for them."

Inside, a curving marble staircase that led to the villa's second floor boasted a delicate wrought-iron banister in a pattern of birds and intertwining leaves. Exceedingly romantic, it had clearly been added during the early years of the twentieth century.

"Allow me, Signora Rossi," Enzo invited, sweeping Laura up in his arms. "My first official act as your husband will be to carry you up the stairs."

Pliant against him, she buried her face against his neck. Incredibly, he was hers—all the fire and melancholy he possessed, all the glinting humor and sweet refuge he was so richly capable of. Together, they'd make a life. Fall asleep each night in each other's arms.

God, but she loved him so.

He put her down in what she guessed was the villa's master bedroom, an airy, spacious off-white chamber dominated by an ornate Venetian bed and floor-to-ceiling lace-curtained windows that had been left partway open to catch the breeze off the water. A bottle of champagne was chilling with two glasses in an antique silver bucket. Massive bouquets of lilies and hydrangeas welcomed them.

"Enzo, I can't believe any of this is happening," Laura said.

"It is, darling. Come... I want to look at you. To touch. Luxuriate. And taste."

Tenderly, as if he were undressing a child, he unbuttoned her aqua silk blouse and slid it down her arms. Her skirt came next, sliding down over her hips and pooling in a heap at her ankles.

"Ah, *cara*... you're so beautiful," he whispered, unclasping her lacy push-up bra and taking possession of her breasts.

The light but erotic pressure of his fingertips as he teased her nipples to taut erectness sent hot currents of longing winging to her depths. Her fantasies, if that was what they were, once more in the ascendant, she had the wild, illogical notion that a promise given centuries earlier was about to be kept. A troth pledged, a love consummated and then abandoned, finally to be reverenced. Deeper than the parameters of their acquaintance might seem to suggest, her need for him resonated with cataclysmic urgency.

Running his hands down her body, Enzo had removed her bikini panties. Naked except for her wedding ring, a wide platinum band he'd ordered from a Milanese jeweler, Laura was completely vulnerable to his gaze. I'm bread for your eating, a honey pot of pleasure awaiting your fingertips, she thought, the oddly archaic diction she'd heard spoken in one of her dreams or visions arising from the deepest part of herself.

She didn't pause to question its source. Or worry what it might portend. "Enzo, please... Take off your things," she begged.

Like her, the man she loved had kicked off his shoes when he set her on her feet. More than willing to do as she asked, he stripped off his linen sport coat, collarless handmade shirt and pleated trousers and tossed them aside on a chair. She gasped with pleasure to learn that he wore nothing beneath them. Tan everywhere but the area usually covered by swimming trunks, he was beautifully made, a generously endowed man in the full flood of desire, erect and ready for her.

Her longing to have him where she wanted him most shot up like a flame doused with kerosene at the evidence of his passion. Reaching out, she grasped and caressed his jutting desire, noting every exquisite vein and ridge and detail before returning her eyes to his face. Her lips parted softly when she saw that his eyes were shut in euphoric concentration.

"You're beautiful, too. Make love to me," she whispered.

With a groan, he lifted her against his body so that her hair fell forward about his face. Instinctively she wrapped her legs around him in a scissors grip. Pushing up her breasts, Enzo set about ravaging them with his mouth. With each damp, sweetly insistent tug, she felt more open, more quintessentially female. I'll be a well for you, she promised him inside her head. Deep and plentiful. As endless as the universe.

He was in her partway, and attempting to penetrate more deeply, as they moved to the bed. They were forced to separate briefly as he laid her against the pillows. A look passed between them, searing in its intensity as they drank in each other's nakedness. Then he was claiming the place between her thighs and covering her, his mat of chest hair brushing her face as he rode high for more intimate contact.

How long they moved together in the big, breeze-scented bed, a white-hot core in the room's light-drenched serenity, Laura couldn't have said. For her, time in a relative sense had ceased to exist. She knew only that she was part of Enzo, and he of her. Tightening and releasing her strong interior muscles, she focused on drawing him deeper with every downstroke. The active welcome she provided didn't just heighten sensation for him; it increased his pressure at the place where she craved it most.

Yes, oh, yes, she thought, consumed and almost incoherent. I want you filling me. Part of me. Taking everything. I'll never get enough.

Straining toward apotheosis, yet greedy to make the moment last, they stripped away the layers of their separateness. Tension built, like a flower opening in time-lapse photography. Each thrust, each loving constriction, brought them closer to releasing it. In a way that was spiritual, as well as physical, their spheres of influence seemed to merge.

With a heart-stopping rush of feeling, the flower's innermost petals opened, positioning them at the brink. Her eyes closed, her thighs spread like wings, Laura let the feeling take her. Up, *up* it lifted her, into vast kingdoms of delight inhabited only by his touch, sensual realms so joyous it was almost beyond her human ability to cope with them.

Abruptly she was jettisoning the last vestiges of control. Rapturous and free, a fierce paroxysm took her, causing her to rock upward from the bed. "Oh . . . oh . . . *oh!*" she cried in little gasps that were as rhythmic as heartbeats as gooseflesh flowed over her thighs and arms and stomach.

A split second later, Enzo joined her, blind with ecstasy as the spasms of his release washed over him. Lovingly she cradled him, in thrall though she still was to her own diminishing jerks and tremors. Heat flooded her cheeks, as if a fire had been kindled there. Her sense of completion, of belonging to the man she loved, was overwhelming.

They slept a little after that, first pulling up the sheet and the elderly contessa's delicately embroidered coverlet. An hour or so later, a discreet tap on the door awoke them. "Pardon me, Signor, Signora Rossi," the houseboy's voice said apologetically. "But it's 5:00 p.m. And I have a family emergency. I must leave. The luggage . . ."

Doubtless the emergency was his girlfriend and a wish to celebrate the weekend with her. "You may bring it in now," Enzo said permissively, after checking to make sure they were decently covered.

Obviously somewhat uncomfortable entering the room where they lay abed, but with a typical Italian's appreciative eye for lovers, the houseboy did as he'd been asked. After he left, Enzo stretched mightily and kissed Laura's cheek. "What do you say we indulge ourselves with some of that champagne and ring for a bite of supper?" he asked. "Afterward, I'll make love to you again."

They pleasured each other twice more that evening, beginning once halfway through their supper of cold meat, bread and a *macedonia di frutta,* and reprising their satisfaction in bed just before they fell asleep. Awash in completion and pleasantly loose in every joint and muscle of her body, Laura sank beyond dreaming. She didn't wake till morning. Sunlight flooded the room, causing the folds of their rumpled sheets to gleam preternaturally white.

When she reached for Enzo, her arms came up empty. A quick look around satisfied her that he wasn't in their bedchamber or its connecting bath. Putting on a robe, Laura went in search of him. She located him in the palazzo's second-floor ballroom, which dominated the center of the house. Naked, barefoot, a pensive silhouette against the lake's brilliance, he was gazing out at the water through one of the ballroom's balustraded French windows.

Was he having second thoughts?

Marching in an even progression across the lake end of the room, the French windows alternated with gilt-framed mirrors in an Empire design. Catching sight of her reflection in one of them, Enzo turned to her and held out his arms.

"Come, sweetheart," he invited with a smile. "Take off your robe. I've been thinking how much I'd like to dance with you without clothing getting in the way."

When they weren't in bed together during the remainder of their visit, they explored the area, driving around the lake and rowing on its meltingly beautiful surface during several lazy afternoons. Trailing a hand in Lake Como's silver ripples as Enzo looked lovingly at her, Laura acknowledged that she'd never known such bliss. Her only uncertainty arose on their last day in the area, after they'd driven across the hills to Luino, on Lake Maggiore, to visit its renowned Wednesday marketplace.

Somehow, amid the confusion of American tourists, Swiss Rolls-Royces and local entrepreneurs hawking prosciutto, fresh bread and grapes, they managed to get separated. Glancing across several stalls of cut flowers, cheese and vegetables, Laura spotted her husband talking to a woman about his age. She was rather pretty in a self-conscious way, with flowing red hair, an ample bosom and slender legs encased in American-style stretch pants. It was obvious from the way they spoke to each other that, whatever their current status, they'd known each other well.

The frown on Enzo's face made it plain that he wasn't particularly glad to see her. After a few emphatic remarks on his part, accompanied by hand gestures, she answered him with a brief retort and walked away. Unbidden, Stefano's claim that Enzo kept a mistress in the Lake District popped into Laura's head.

I won't think about what he said, she vowed, pushing down the rush of jealousy the memory evoked. It doesn't matter whether Stefano was right or not. The past is finished. I needn't worry about it. When they were reunited, Enzo didn't mention the incident. And she didn't ask him about it. His strong right arm about her waist and the tender kiss he placed on her mouth were all the reassurance she wanted.

They returned to the Villa Voglia the following afternoon to learn that Paolo had scarcely missed their presence. According to Anna, Michele had been teaching him to play *bocce* and ride Guido, a docile, elderly pony he'd borrowed from one of the neighbors. Emilia had done her part by tutoring the boy in Italian. As his primary caretaker, Anna had bandaged a skinned knee and read numerous bedtime stories.

Much as his new family had loved and spoiled him, however, he was glad to see his mother. To Laura's satisfaction, Cristina and Vittorio had returned to Turin the day before, giving her and Enzo a wide berth. I suppose we'll have to see them there, however their lawsuit turns out, she thought. Just not too often, I hope.

The company at the dinner table that night was relaxed and serene, in distinct contrast to Laura's first meal in the Rossi household. To her, Anna appeared far happier than she had on that occasion, despite Umberto's death. Even Emilia, ramrod-straight in her black mourning dress, appeared relatively content. She gazed at Paolo with love and smiled faintly but indulgently at the affectionate way Enzo touched Laura's shoulder at one point for emphasis. Only Stefano, who had arrived late, seemed to resent their obvious happiness.

After supper, Laura took Paolo for a walk while Enzo disappeared into his study to go over some neglected paperwork. When she asked her son if he missed his life in Chicago, he shrugged with the flair of an Italian native.

"It was okay there, Mom," he allowed. "Josie was a cool baby-sitter. But I like Grandmother Anna better. We aren't going back, are we? Grandmother Emilia says we're going to live here permanently."

Laura's mouth curved. She was beginning to develop a fondness for the Rossi matriarch. "Grandmother Emilia is right," she said. "But we'll be visiting Chicago... and perhaps New York... fairly regularly. I'll still be working with Aunt Carol, you know. Besides... Gram and Grampa Wilson will expect it."

She was about to rejoin Enzo after putting Paolo to bed when Stefano appeared in the upstairs hall. "Will you give me a minute, sister-in-law?" he asked.

Afraid of what he'd say, that somehow it would undermine her happiness, Laura shrank from him with distaste.

"There's something you ought to know," he insisted. "You probably don't believe it. But I have your best interests at heart."

It would be the usual poison, she guessed. Yet perhaps she ought to listen. She might learn something. Enzo had a right to know what kind of lies his half brother was spreading about him.

"All right," she said warily, trying to blunt the expression of dislike on her face.

He didn't waste any time getting to the point. "Remember the woman Enzo met in the market at Luino?" he asked. "She's the mistress I spoke about."

More in love with Enzo than she'd thought possible a short time earlier, Laura found it extremely distasteful to imagine him making love to another woman. She was even more disturbed by her own feelings of insecurity. What if the woman he saw in Luino *is* a former lover? she tried to tell herself. A brief conversation with someone who used to be important to him isn't cause for distress. Enzo's done nothing whatever to make me distrust him.

"Sorry to disappoint you, Stefano, but I'm not the jealous type," she retorted, feeling as if she'd missed something, but unable to fasten on what it was.

The family interloper raised a quizzical brow. "Not even if the two of them made plans to meet?"

Laura felt as if an elevator had plunged several stories to hit bottom in the pit of her stomach. A moment later, she came partway to her senses. "I don't believe you," she said. "How could you possibly know about something like that? In fact, who told you about Enzo running into that woman in the first place? I know I didn't. And I doubt if Enzo would confide in you."

Instead of appearing cornered, Stefano gave a satisfied little shrug. "She phoned me," he related. "We've kept in touch. She wanted to know what kind of marriage my brother had contracted that he's still interested in her."

Chapter Eleven

Was it possible Stefano was telling the truth? For him to have learned about the incident at all, she realized, the woman had to have contacted him. He couldn't have done so any other way since he'd stayed at the estate. Once perceived, that simple fact was like a battering ram, assailing her trust in Enzo at its foundation. Though she tried to push them down, all her former questions about him erupted again. Had he married her simply to gain control of Paolo's stock in Rossi Motorworks? And please Emilia in the bargain? Or did he truly care for her? Despite the passionate, tender love they'd shared, did he lust after another woman's body?

Aside from hiring a detective to investigate, there was only one way to find out the truth. She'd ask. Turning her back on Stefano without another word, she raced downstairs and threw open the door of Enzo's study.

He was listening to opera on the radio and writing in a

large, old-fashioned checkbook. "Something wrong, *cara?*" he asked, glancing at her over the rims of his reading glasses.

Resting her palms on his leather-topped desk, she disgorged Stefano's accusations in a rush. Nothing in her manner discounted them. It was as if she were flinging them in his face.

"He says the woman phoned him," she concluded. "Supposedly she wanted to know what kind of marriage you'd gotten yourself into, if you were eager to arrange an assignation with her before the ink was dry on our wedding license!"

With each word that fell from her mouth, Enzo's expression grew more thunderous. It's happening again, he thought, overcome with rage and disillusionment. The jealousy. And the venom. Eight years ago he slept with my fiancée so that I'd break off my wedding plans. Now that I've finally found the wife I've always wanted, he torpedoes her trust.

True, the loss of Luciana Paraggi, the wealthy Milanese socialite he'd been engaged to marry at the age of thirty, had turned out to be a blessing. But he'd never forgiven his half brother the humiliation and hurt. With Laura, of course, it was a completely different situation. She hadn't cheated on him. Yet apparently she thought him capable of doing her that injury—while they were still on their honeymoon! Her readiness to believe Stefano's lies cut him to the quick.

She was waiting for an answer, some kind of explanation. Well, he'd be damned if he'd give her one. "Is that it?" he asked, keeping his voice tightly controlled.

Laura nodded. Guilt and uncertainty were raising their ugly heads. Had she made a terrible mistake?

His manner hard and unyielding, Enzo returned his attention to his checkbook.

"Aren't you going to say something?" she asked.

The question shattered the remnants of his self-control. "What do you *want* me to say?" he demanded furiously, leaping to his feet and catching hold of her by the wrists. "That it's not so? As far as I'm concerned, you're welcome to think whatever you damn well please!"

His fingers were biting into her flesh, causing her to wince with discomfort. With a cry of anguish, she pulled free of him and ran out of the room. The clatter of her heels against the *sala*'s inlaid marble tiles receded as she rushed out into the loggia and down the villa's front steps.

Immobilized by anger and his fear of what it might make him do if he took even the most tentative action, Enzo was standing exactly as she'd left him when Anna spoke to him from the open door to an adjoining room. Usually so reticent about interfering in the affairs of others, she was clearly overwrought. "Forgive me, son," she begged, her soft voice taut with urgency. "I couldn't help overhearing part of your conversation with Laura. I know you don't believe in psychic foreboding, but I beg you to pay attention to mine. I'm convinced something awful will happen if you don't go after her...."

Never one to take his mother's premonitions seriously, or to set much store in her affinity with psychic portents, Enzo was suddenly disposed to believe her. Tearing his anguished gaze from her worried one, he ran after the infuriatingly independent American he'd come to love.

Stumbling past the boundary of the formal garden, Laura found herself on the gravel path to the stable. Unlit, its dark, barely differentiated shape loomed ahead. She felt drawn there as if by a magnet. Abruptly the memory of her regression at Alice Kidwell's hands assailed her. No, she thought. *No.* You can't do this. It's dangerous.

There didn't seem to be any turning back. Before she fully realized what was happening, her ears had begun to buzz.

Like the gallery at the Art Institute where she'd seen the first
Renaissance portrait, the plantings and outbuildings of the
Rossi estate seemed to dissolve into shining fragments.

When the sensation passed, the stable was still there, built
solidly of stone, in front of her. Strangely, its weathered
surface appeared rejuvenated. The creepers that had covered it had disappeared. Several of the villa's other outbuildings seemed to have vanished without a trace.

Mesmerized, she glanced down at her sleeves, and then at
the remainder of her clothing. It seemed she was dressed
differently, too. Instead of her flowered silk skirt and
matching rose-colored sweater, she was wearing a high-
waisted bottle-green velvet gown. Its skirt narrowly missed
trailing in the dirt of a path that seemed to have altered beneath her feet.

With the discovery, her identity faded from her grasp. It
became clear to her that she wasn't "Laura" at all, but a
younger woman named Rafaella—one who'd lived in Italy's Piedmont area all her life and heard only passing ref-
erences to a new land across the ocean. Things such as the
exploration of the world meant nothing to her. She was on
her way to the stable to...to...check on her favorite mare's
new colt.

She could smell the pungent aroma of horseflesh, inhale
the hay's sun-ripened sweetness, hear the contented sound
of the mare blowing softly to her knobby-kneed offspring
as she entered the stable's shadowy interior. Seconds later
her heart hammered against her ribs as fierce arms imprisoned her and a man's hand was clapped over her mouth.

Was her attacker some ruffian who'd wandered onto the
villa property? Or Vicenzo Uccelli, the intense, dark-eyed
cousin she'd wed several months earlier? He was due back
from Firenze, where he'd gone to settle an estate, at any
moment.

The latter, she prayed with all her strength.

"Cenzo, please . . . you're hurting me!" she protested.

She realized her mistake as a billow of scarlet curled about her ankles. Unbelievable though it might seem, her captor was none other than Vicenzo's sinister identical twin, Giulio Cardinal Uccelli, a prince of the church, courtesy of his family's wealth and prominence.

"Not him . . . *me*," he said in his sinuous, somehow threatening voice. "Are you disappointed?"

He'd been watching her for weeks, paying ever more frequent visits to the estate in his brother's absence. Each time he'd appeared, he'd paid undue attention to her. And she'd grown more nervous. On one recent occasion when they'd been alone in the garden, he'd had the audacity to ask her if she was pregnant.

Out of respect for his position, if not for him as a person, she'd confessed she wasn't, yet. Well aware that Vicenzo was the last of his line and desperately wanted an heir, she'd hoped to surprise her husband with different news. As things stood, the best she'd be able to offer him on his return was her willingness to redouble their efforts.

"Your . . . Eminence," she stammered now as Giulio relaxed his hold slightly. "I don't understand . . . what you want of me."

"Ah, but I think you do, Rafaella."

Controlling yet almost negligent as he exercised his superior strength, Giulio turned her around to face him. To her dismay, the lust she'd secretly suspected lay in his heart was shining nakedly on his face.

"Please," she begged, fear rising in an ice-cold flood. "Let me go. You're a man of God. And I'm your brother's wife. It isn't right for us to be this intimate."

Her captor responded with a smile—twisted as a result of the boyhood scar that puckered his left cheek. "Why should Vicenzo know your sweetness, your passion . . . father the next heir to Villa Voglia . . . while I'm condemned to a life of prayer and chastity?'' he demanded. "He and I are one, two sides of a single coin. We were born of the same parents, just a few minutes apart.''

Glancing around as he emerged from the loggia, Enzo didn't see Laura anywhere. Had she gone to the garage and commandeered one of the family vehicles, taking a key from the rack of spares hanging there? Or was she walking, briskly, on the path to the little woods where Michele hunted for truffles, trying to regain her composure and her trust in him?

He knew she wouldn't leave him permanently without her little boy. Nor would she get very far without money or a passport. Uncertain which way to turn, he spotted the old gardener, who was out with his mongrel dog for an evening constitutional.

"Michele . . . have you seen my wife?'' he asked.

The old man nodded. "She went toward the stable, Signor Enzo.''

"Grazie."

His sense of urgency intensifying, he started after her. Suddenly, as he neared the stable, his shoes crunching gravel underfoot, he staggered at the onset of a blinding headache. From the initial stabs of pain, he could tell it would be one of his worst. Tempted to turn back and try to contain the onslaught by downing his prescribed pain medication, he remembered Anna's warning. *I have to find Laura,* he thought.

His head throbbing more violently by the moment, he hurried forward and entered the stable through a half-open door. As he did so, his ears began to ring. He felt his equilibrium falter, as if he might pass out on the spot. I can't afford to let that happen, he thought.

A moment later, fainting was the last thing on his mind. Seemingly so solid and tranquil, the peaceful tableau of the

Rossi horses munching hay in the new stalls Stefano had ordered built several months earlier dissolved into a spangled mosaic of light and shadow. When he could focus again, he was horrified at the scene that met his eyes. His brother, Stefano...no, *Giulio*...was making forcible advances to the wife of his body.

Not pausing to question their disheveled sixteenth-century garb, his own similar transformation or the archaic turn of phrase that had crept so naturally into his thoughts, he flung himself atop his brother, pulling Giulio from the struggling young woman who'd attempted to defend her honor by raking his face with her fingernails.

Unexpectedly he caught the glint of a knife. The flash of perception was followed by a sharp stab of pain in his abdomen. "No!" a woman screamed. "Please, God...don't let him die!" His breathing ragged, he staggered backward. When he clutched at his stomach, in an attempt to quell his suffering, his hands came away covered with blood. Giulio had murdered him! A prisoner of his quivering, terribly violated flesh, he would die at any moment. As he collapsed on the stable's hay-strewn floor, an awareness of his present life seemed to overlap the situation in which he found himself. Incredibly, the scene he was playing out was that of his nightmare. Yet, contrary to the ingrained belief of his psyche, he'd done no murder. The blood that covered his hands was his own.

In the same flash of insight, he was aware of events still to come from a sixteenth-century perspective. If he couldn't summon the strength to stop Giulio's rape of the woman who once again struggled in his clutches, she'd conceive a child. Hustled off to a convent, she'd die in childbirth. Though he, as Vicenzo, would live to a bitter old age and see Giulio ruined for his crime, the retribution he craved wouldn't be swift. A church tribunal, not the ducal court in

Turin, would try the case. Giulio would declare he was defending Rafaella from a bestial attack by her husband.

Pregnant with Giulio's child and hidden away behind convent walls, the young woman known as Rafaella wouldn't be allowed to testify. Several of Giulio's fellow cardinals would intercede on his behalf. Unwilling to besmirch the church's reputation by convicting him, the judges would let him go.

With a superhuman effort, the man he'd become surmounted the weakness that flowed from his wound and flung himself on Giulio a second time. Moments later, he found himself back in the late twentieth century. He was kneeling, dazed, on the floor of the Villa Voglia stable, with Laura clutched against his chest.

"Enzo...darling...thank God you're all right," she wept, showering his face with kisses.

"He never actually touched me."

The moment the words were out of his mouth, Enzo realized they applied to the present, not the horrible scenario from the past in which they'd both participated. From their current perspective, there was no "he," no third party, in the stable with them.

"Were you...*there?*" he asked, not entirely sure he could justify the word's use, as they hadn't changed location. "Did you see—"

She nodded. "Everything. Stefano stabbed you. He was trying to rape me. Except it wasn't Stefano. It was . . ."

"Giulio Cardinal Uccelli. The prelate . . ."

"In the Turin portrait."

"Yes."

"*You* were the man with the gloves, in the velvet doublet."

"I don't understand."

She hadn't told him of the Art Institute portrait, or her powerful reaction to it. Safe from harm in his embrace, she remedied that lapse, describing her Renaissance nobleman and telling him of her dizzy spells.

He stared at her in amazement. "The same kind of thing happened to *me,* on my way here."

She nestled closer. "I should have confided in you from the beginning."

"I wish you *had,* sweetheart. We might have been able to sidestep some of the trauma we experienced tonight."

"Maybe. Somehow I doubt it. Strange as it may seem, I'm convinced we were meant to go through that struggle with Giulio.... lay it finally to rest."

They had a lot to talk about. Humbled by the realization that her doubts had nearly spawned disastrous consequences, Laura declared herself uninterested in an explanation of the tableau at the Luino market.

"I behaved like a fool, swallowing Stefano's poison wholesale that way," she admitted. "Please believe me when I say I have no curiosity about that woman or your conversation with her. Instead of wasting time talking about it, let's ask your grandmother if she knows any historical details."

Her mention of Emilia called to mind the concern on Anna's face. By now, Enzo guessed, his mother was probably frantic. They could talk about Luciana and his surprise encounter with her in Luino later.

"Let's go, then," he urged, tugging Laura to her feet. "My mother heard you run out, and she was very worried about you. I'd like to set her mind at rest."

As they neared the villa by means of the gravel path that, a short time earlier, had led them into the trauma of the distant past, they saw Anna hovering by the loggia entrance.

"Thank God you're all right!" she exclaimed, coming partway down the steps to meet them. "I've rung for coffee. If you can abide a mother's meddling, I'm eager to hear if anything unusual transpired."

Enzo glanced at Laura.

"Actually, something did," Laura admitted. "I'll be happy to tell you all about it, if Enzo doesn't mind."

Keenly attuned to everything that went on at the villa, Emilia met them in the *sala* before they could go in search of her. "Come...join me in my sitting room," she said, scanning their faces. "I've asked that the coffee Anna ordered be brought to us there."

"Where's Stefano?" Enzo asked as Gemma brought in a steaming china pot and filled their coffee cups.

Anna couldn't tell him. But Emilia could. At least she could vouch for the fact that he wasn't on the villa grounds. "He left a good half hour ago," she said. "I saw his car pull out and turn toward Asti."

Laura and Enzo looked at each other. Apparently, though in a sense he'd instigated it, Stefano hadn't shared their riveting experience at the stable. For him, the past, disastrous connection they were convinced they'd uncovered had remained shrouded in mist.

"He may have been affected by the past...." Enzo speculated.

Part of him now, in a way she'd only longed to be before, Laura completed the sentence. "But he wasn't fated to relive it as we did."

Glancing from her grandson to Laura and back again with penetrating curiosity, Emilia demanded to know what was going on. They took turns telling her, leaving out the argument Anna had overheard, and acknowledging their joint belief that they'd traveled back in time to a previous existence.

The Rossi matriarch's interest—and Anna's—quickened when Enzo mentioned the similarity of Laura's sixteenth-century attacker to the churchman depicted in the Turin portrait. Laura followed with a description of what had happened to her at the Art Institute.

"When we saw Giulio's portrait in Turin, I though it might represent the man whose likeness I saw in Chicago at a somewhat later age," she told her husband. "I realize now I was mistaken. It must have depicted *you,* as Vicenzo, darling. Otherwise, I doubt I'd have felt such a deep attraction to its subject."

As they continued to drink their coffee, Enzo dared for the first time to speak of his nightmares and persistent headaches in his grandmother's presence. The censure he'd expected wasn't forthcoming. In like manner, Laura recapped the dizzy spells she'd suffered since coming to Italy. Both they and the symptoms Enzo had suffered were likely to stop now, she speculated.

"Previously, the idea of past lives was foreign to my thinking," Enzo admitted when finally she ran out of words. "Yet there seems to be no other rational explanation for what we shared. Can you shed any further light on the historical characters into whose lives we stumbled, Grandmother?"

She was able to tell them a bit more than he'd expected. "Both Cardinal Uccelli and the Vicenzo of whom you speak were real people," she said. "Born identical twins, they were the last generation of Uccellis to live at the Villa Voglia.

"As the firstborn son, Vicenzo was the villa's rightful heir. That left Giulio with slender means, at best. The story goes that their father forced him to dedicate his life to the church. In keeping with the experience you describe, there was a scandal involving Giulio and Vicenzo's recent bride. Officially exonerated of raping her, Giulio remained under a cloud of suspicion. His career in the church was effectively finished. The wife, whose name I can't recall at the moment, became pregnant... either by some other man while her husband was away, or forcibly by Giulio, as Vicenzo insisted. She was sent to a convent, where she died in childbirth. Her infant perished with her.''

Again Laura and her husband traded glances. At last I understand the danger I felt, she thought. I associated it with Enzo, while all along Stefano... the echoes of Giulio in him... was its radiating source. At the same time, she could better understand her reluctance to rely on Enzo's support. Outraged over the blow done to his honor, his sixteenth-century self had abandoned her.

"What happened to Vicenzo after the trial and his wife's death?" she asked.

Emilia's blue-veined hands lightly framed her coffee cup. "He didn't marry again. Supposedly he lived here at the villa as a widower until his death. Afterward, it was sold by his heirs. My late husband's grandfather bought it from a noble Lombard family in 1887. As you know, Enzo, though perhaps Laura does not, the Rossi family is distantly descended from the Uccelli twins' younger sister, Lucia Maddelena, who married a prosperous Milanese landowner."

Inevitably the discussion kept returning to the subject of past lives, as if drawn to it by a magnet. "I don't see why we were hurled backward in time, if that's what happened," Enzo said. "We didn't manage to change anything."

"For myself, *I* wish I'd asked you about the Uccellis earlier," Laura interjected. "We might have been spared all that anguish."

Silent until now, Anna leaned forward in her chair. "If I might be permitted..." she said.

Everyone, including her frail but imposing mother-in-law, turned to her in surprise.

"It's my belief that, if you go back in time," Anna said earnestly, "you can't alter what happened...just your soul memory of it. Yet perhaps that's enough, if it exorcises demons... reassures the person you are in the present tense. Maybe the emotional trauma you were forced to undergo was necessary to lay the past to rest. Intellectual knowing wouldn't have been enough.''

Briefly the room was quiet enough to hear a pin drop as everyone absorbed her diffidently offered wisdom. I have a feeling she's right, Enzo thought. I'd be willing to bet I've seen the last of my nightmares. Of course, only time will tell.

At last Emilia stirred. ''It's past my bedtime, children,'' she said, including Anna in that grouping, though she was in her early sixties. ''I suggest we continue our discussion at the breakfast table.''

Always dutiful, Anna offered to accompany her mother-in-law upstairs. Laura and Enzo followed them. It would be their first night as man and wife at the Villa Voglia. Aware he'd been emotionally rough on Laura when she accosted him in his office, and sensitive to the fact that she had been the victim of undue violence in the past-life scenario they'd just enacted, Enzo was reluctant to exert additional pressure on her. Yet he didn't want Stefano's poison to linger in her thinking.

''About the rendezvous I was supposed to be planning with the woman I met in Luino...'' he said as they entered his former bachelor quarters.

Her distress was immediate. ''Please, let's just forget it,'' she implored. ''I shouldn't even have mentioned it to you.''

Lovingly Enzo pulled her close. ''We've probably known each other for centuries,'' he said. ''But not very well in this one yet, it seems.''

Her reply was muffled against his shirt.

''Come to bed with me and talk,'' he said.

Nestled in Enzo's arms, with moonlight splashing across the bed covers and the scent of late-blooming lilies from Michele's garden perfuming the air, Laura listened as Enzo explained that the redhead he'd spoken with in Luino was none other than his former fiancée, the woman who'd betrayed him with his half brother.

"I'm not particularly surprised she contacted him to say she'd run into me," he revealed. "They were lovers, after all, though he lost interest in her the moment I did. My engagement to her was a mistake from the beginning . . . one I managed to rectify before it was too late. Admittedly, she still phones me sometimes, though I've never demonstrated any interest. Now that I have *you*, she'd be insane to think I would."

His words had the ring of truth. After thirty-three years, give or take a few centuries, Laura was exactly where she belonged. "Make love to me," she whispered.

Enzo was more than willing. They'd stripped off their clothing before getting into bed, and no buttons or zippers stood in the way. In what seemed only seconds, she was burning to ashes with his kisses, sheltering him deep in the well of her need for him.

As she rose up from the bed to meet him and he cried aloud in his ecstasy, their very souls seemed to merge. It was as if, in evoking each other's total abandonment, they'd put paid to an ancient debt. Henceforth, the way would be clear for unlimited love and understanding and trust.

Quieting, they talked a little more about their experience. Though she couldn't be sure, Laura was convinced she wouldn't suffer again from the buzzing in her ears that had so dismayed her, or glimpse unwanted tableaux from the past. To her, the door to the previous lifetime she'd shared with Enzo seemed firmly shut. In a way, she regretted it.

"I don't suppose we'll ever know if Vicenzo lamented abandoning Rafaella to her fate," she said, a trifle wistfully.

Enzo agreed. "You know," he added, "it's incredible to me that, if he loved her as I believe he did, the man I was would let the woman you were go off to a convent. What matter that she was carrying his brother's child? She didn't ask to be in that situation. She wanted *his*. Like me, apparently, he had a lot to learn. I'm just so grateful you'd marry me again . . . and give our love another chance.''

Generous in their happiness, they came to a meeting of the minds about a surprising topic as they lay tangled up together beneath Enzo's down coverlet. In their opinion, much of Stefano's jealousy and ill will flowed from his lack of acceptance. Though he might squander the opportunity, they'd do their best to make him feel more included— whether or not he persisted in his proposed lawsuit.

"It'll be difficult . . . especially for me," Enzo acknowledged, "given our history. But I might be able manage it."

"The same thing goes for Cristina, where I'm concerned," Laura replied. "I'll try not to be angry at her, even if she follows through on her threats. Secure in your love, I feel my generosity spilling over."

Like his siblings, Guy was also in their thoughts.

"Do you think it's possible," Enzo asked softly, "that the tug of past events and his family connection to me, and thus to the man I once was, drew you to him when you met?"

Laura thought about it a moment. "I really don't know," she acknowledged at last. "All I can say is that I loved Guy very much. I'll always view my life with him as a separate and positive thing."

Incredibly, he understood.

Relaxed as it was, their heart-to-heart talk dispelled the languor that had followed their lovemaking, and they found themselves wanting each other again. More deeply in love than ever because of the abiding trust they'd begun to build, they set a second seal on the beginning of their present life together.

* * * * *

LAURA VAN WORMER

❦❦❦ ★ ❦❦❦

Just for the Summer

Nothing prepares Mary Liz for the summer she spends in
the moneyed town of East Hampton, Long Island. From
the death of one of their own, Mary Liz realises that these
stunningly beautiful people have some of the ugliest
agendas in the world.

*"Van Wormer,...has the glamorama Hampton's scene down to
a T. (Just for the Summer is) as voyeuristic as it is fun."*
—Kirkus Reviews

1-55166-439-9
AVAILABLE FROM JUNE 1998

MIRA®

MILLS & BOON®

Next Month's Romances

♡

Each month you can choose from a wide variety of romance novels from Mills & Boon®. Below are the new titles to look out for next month from the Presents™ and Enchanted™ series.

Presents™

JOINED BY MARRIAGE	Carole Mortimer
THE MARRIAGE SURRENDER	Michelle Reid
FORBIDDEN PLEASURE	Robyn Donald
IN BED WITH A STRANGER	Lindsay Armstrong
A HUSBAND'S PRICE	Diana Hamilton
GIRL TROUBLE	Sandra Field
DANTE'S TWINS	Catherine Spencer
SUMMER SEDUCTION	Daphne Clair

Enchanted™

NANNY BY CHANCE	Betty Neels
GABRIEL'S MISSION	Margaret Way
THE TWENTY-FOUR-HOUR BRIDE	Day Leclaire
THE DADDY TRAP	Leigh Michaels
BIRTHDAY BRIDE	Jessica Hart
THE PRINCESS AND THE PLAYBOY	Valerie Parv
WANTED: PERFECT PARTNER	Debbie Macomber
SHOWDOWN!	Ruth Jean Dale

On sale from 13th July 1998

H1 9806

Available at most branches of
WH Smith, John Menzies, Martins, Tesco,
Asda, Volume One, Sainsbury and Safeway

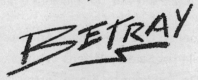
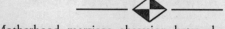

Barbara DELINSKY

THE DREAM UNFOLDS

Even adversaries can become lovers

Gideon Lowe and Christine Gillette shared a dream—
to develop Crosslyn Rise into an elegant apartment
complex on the Atlantic coast. That dream is all they
share. But lust can get around misconceptions and
even adversaries can become lovers.

"(An author) of sensitivity and style."

—Publishers Weekly

1-55166-161-6
AVAILABLE FROM JUNE 1998

SPOT THE DIFFERENCE

Spot all ten differences between the two pictures featured below and you could win a year's supply of Mills & Boon® books—FREE! When you're finished, simply complete the coupon overleaf and send it to us by 31st December 1998. The first five correct entries will each win a year's subscription to the Mills & Boon series of their choice. What could be easier?

Please turn over for details of how to enter ⇨

F8C

HOW TO ENTER

Simply study the two pictures overleaf. They may at first glance appear the same but look closely and you should start to see the differences. There are ten to find in total, so circle them as you go on the second picture. Finally, fill in the coupon below and pop this page into an envelope and post it today. Don't forget you could win a year's supply of Mills & Boon® books—you don't even need to pay for a stamp!

Mills & Boon Spot the Difference Competition
FREEPOST CN81, Croydon, Surrey, CR9 3WZ
EIRE readers: (please affix stamp) PO Box 4546, Dublin 24.

Please tick the series you would like to receive if you are one of the lucky winners

Presents™ ❑ Enchanted™ ❑ Medical Romance™ ❑
Historical Romance™ ❑ Temptation® ❑

Are you a Reader Service™ subscriber?   Yes ❑   No ❑

Ms/Mrs/Miss/Mr ....Initials ....
(BLOCK CAPITALS PLEASE)

Surname...

Address ....

....

.............................Postcode...........................

(I am over 18 years of age)   F8C

Closing date for entries is 31st December 1998.
One application per household. Competition open to residents of the UK and Ireland only. You may be mailed with offers from other reputable companies as a result of this application. If you would prefer not to receive such offers, please tick this box. ❑

Mills & Boon is a registered trademark owned by Harlequin Mills & Boon Limited.

EMILIE RICHARDS

RUNAWAY

Runaway **is the first of an intriguing trilogy.**

Krista Jensen is desperate. Desperate enough to pose as a young
prostitute and walk the narrow alley ways of New Orleans.
So it's with relief that Krista finds herself a protector in
the form of Jess Cantrell. Grateful for his help,
she isn't sure she can trust him.

Trusting the wrong man could prove fatal.

1-55166-398-8
AVAILABLE FROM JUNE 1998

Penny Jordan

COLLECTOR'S EDITION

The *Penny Jordan Collector's Edition* is
a selection of her most popular stories,
published in beautifully designed volumes
for you to collect and cherish.

*Available from Tesco, Asda, WH Smith, John Menzies,
Martins and all good paperback stockists, at £3.10 each -
or the special price of £2.80 if you use the coupon below.
On sale from 1st June 1998.*

Valid only in the UK & Eire against purchases made in retail outlets and not in conjunction with any Reader Service or other offer.

30ᵖ OFF

COUPON

VALID UNTIL: 31.8.1998

PENNY JORDAN COLLECTOR'S EDITION

To the Customer: This coupon can be used in part payment for a copy of PENNY JORDAN COLLECTOR'S EDITION. Only one coupon can be used against each copy purchased. Valid only in the UK & Eire against purchases made in retail outlets and not in conjunction with any Reader Service or other offer. Please do not attempt to redeem this coupon against any other product as refusal to accept may cause embarrassment and delay at the checkout.

To the Retailer: Harlequin Mills & Boon will redeem this coupon at face value provided only that it has been taken in part payment for any book in the PENNY JORDAN COLLECTOR'S EDITION. The company reserves the right to refuse payment against misredeemed coupons. Please submit coupons to: Harlequin Mills & Boon Ltd. NCH Dept 730, Corby, Northants NN17 1NN.

9 904170 250306 >

0472 01316